PINNED

Keeping his eyes on the big man before him, Fargo reached back, plucked the coin pouch off the bar, and thrust it against the man's chest, the coins clinking around inside.

The freighter dropped his gaze to the pouch, returned it to Fargo.

The Trailsman held the man's hard glare.

The freighter lurched forward, red-faced, swinging his ham-sized right fist toward Fargo's face.

The Trailsman, anticipating the punch, grabbed the man's wrist and, pivoting, bulled the man's back against the bar and thrust the man's hand out across the planks. Pressing his own back against the man's chest, wedging him against the bar, Fargo reached out with his free hand, plucked the knife from the bar top, and slammed it through the freighter's open palm and into the wood. . . .

THE
TRAILSMAN
#316

BEYOND
SQUAW CREEK

by

Jon Sharpe

A SIGNET BOOK

SIGNET
Published by New American Library, a division of
Penguin Group (USA) Inc., 375 Hudson Street,
New York, New York 10014, USA
Penguin Group (Canada), 90 Eglinton Avenue East, Suite 700, Toronto,
Ontario M4P 2Y3, Canada (a division of Pearson Penguin Canada Inc.)
Penguin Books Ltd., 80 Strand, London WC2R 0RL, England
Penguin Ireland, 25 St. Stephen's Green, Dublin 2,
Ireland (a division of Penguin Books Ltd.)
Penguin Group (Australia), 250 Camberwell Road, Camberwell, Victoria 3124,
Australia (a division of Pearson Australia Group Pty. Ltd.)
Penguin Books India Pvt. Ltd., 11 Community Centre, Panchsheel Park,
New Delhi - 110 017, India
Penguin Group (NZ), 67 Apollo Drive, Rosedale, North Shore 0632,
New Zealand (a division of Pearson New Zealand Ltd.)
Penguin Books (South Africa) (Pty.) Ltd., 24 Sturdee Avenue,
Rosebank, Johannesburg 2196, South Africa

Penguin Books Ltd., Registered Offices:
80 Strand, London WC2R 0RL, England

First published by Signet, an imprint of New American Library,
a division of Penguin Group (USA) Inc.

First Printing, February 2008
10 9 8 7 6 5 4 3 2 1

The first chapter of this book previously appeared in *Missouri Manhunt*, the
three hundred fifteenth volume in this series.

The Trailsman

Beginnings . . . they bend the tree and they mark the man. Skye Fargo was born when he was eighteen. Terror was his midwife, vengeance his first cry. Killing spawned Skye Fargo, ruthless, cold-blooded murder. Out of the acrid smoke of gunpowder still hanging in the air, he rose, cried out a promise never forgotten.

The Trailsman they began to call him all across the West: searcher, scout, hunter, the man who could see where others only looked, his skills for hire but not his soul, the man who lived each day to the fullest, yet trailed each tomorrow. Skye Fargo, the Trailsman, the seeker who could take the wildness of a land and the wanting of a woman and make them his own.

Dakota Territory, 1860—where wolves prowl in high grasses and death hides just beyond the horizon.

1

"I bet you could do a lot of damage with that thing—couldn't you, Mr. Fargo?" the major's daughter asked.

Skye Fargo ran his lake blue eyes across the girl's willowy frame, the proud breasts pushing up from the shirtwaist of her traveling dress—pale and lightly freckled and sheathing a small jade cameo, the same green of her eyes, hanging by a gold chain. Her shirtwaists had been getting tighter and tighter over the past few days since the party had left Fort Mandan, exposing more and more of her cleavage.

The stagecoach was parked in a canyon of White-Tail Creek, in western Dakota Territory. Valeria Howard sat in a canvas chair before the stage's left front wheel, holding a parasol over her regal head of bright red hair. Fargo sat on the ground ten feet away from her, his back to a boulder, sharpening his Arkansas toothpick on the whetstone perched on his thigh.

The soldiers escorting the stage from Fort Mandan had taken their own mounts and the stage's four-horse hitch down to the creek for water.

"Miss Howard, you got no idea," Fargo said.

Her nose wrinkled and her jade eyes glinted snootily as she continued staring at the knife on his thigh. "A rather uncouth customer, aren't you?"

"Wanna see?"

"Do I want to see *what*?"

"How much damage I can do with this thing."

Fargo followed her smoky gaze to his lap then glanced up at her, curling his upper lip. "The knife *is* the . . . uh . . . *thing* we're talking about, isn't it, Miss Howard?"

Her eyes snapped up, and a flush rose in her cream cheeks. She opened her mouth to speak but only gasped when Fargo snapped up the toothpick suddenly, and sent the six inches of razor-edged, bone-handled steel careening through the air in front of her.

She recoiled as the knife whistled past her, missing the sleeve of her muslin blouse by a half inch, to cleave the gap between two wheel spokes and bury itself, hilt deep, in one of the two brown eyes staring out from behind the hub. The Indian made a gagging sound as his head snapped back, lower jaw dropping, the remaining eye wide open.

As the girl fell over in her chair, her feathered, lemon yellow hat tumbling off her shoulder, Fargo bounded onto his knees and clawed his Colt .44 from its holster. He aimed quickly at one of the two Indians bounding onto the stage's roof from the other side, and fired.

The bullet plunked through the medicine pouch dangling from the neck of the brave standing near the driver's box. As the brave screamed and pitched backward off the coach, throwing his bow and arrow over his head, the second brave leaped forward atop a steamer trunk, gave a savage war cry, and loosed an arrow.

The feathered missile shaved a couple of whiskers

from Fargo's right cheek as it whistled past his ear to clatter against the sandstone scarp behind him.

Fargo triggered the Colt twice, the slugs hammering into the brave's neck and breastbone, pinwheeling him off the coach in twin streams of geysering blood.

"Stay down!" Fargo hurdled Valeria Howard, cowering on the ground beside her overturned chair, and climbed the stage to the driver's box.

Holding the cocked Colt in his right hand, he leaped onto the wooden seat, and then from the seat to the sandstone wall on the other side of the stage, his boots finding a narrow ledge while his left hand reached for a gnarled cedar.

As he looked up and right, a brave peered down at him from behind a thumb of rock, his face streaked with yellow and ocher war designs, eyes wide with rage. The brave raised a feathered war lance but before he could cock his throwing arm, Fargo drilled a round through his forehead, blowing him back off the scarp with a grunt, the lance clattering down the rocks behind him.

Clinging to the gnarled cedar, the .44 smoking in his right hand, the man known as the Trailsman turned to peer south through a break in the opposite canyon wall.

Since just after he'd cleaved the first buck's head with his Arkansas toothpick, he'd heard sporadic gunfire and war whoops from the direction of the creek. Through the cottonwoods lining the stream, he spied smoke puffs, prancing horses, and soldiers scrambling to repel the Indians attacking from the creek's far side. Several of the savages rode horses and triggered pistols and repeating rifles while others, running afoot, loosed arrows and heaved war lances.

The soldiers returned fire while trying to hold the reins of their frightened bays.

As Fargo watched, several soldiers and cavalry mounts went down screaming, and the Indians continued charging, whooping, and shooting. Only nine soldiers had been assigned to the stagecoach carrying not only the beautiful daughter of Major Howard, the commander of Fort Clark, but two army surveyors detailed to Fort Clark to plot the site of a planned sister fort near the mouth of the Wolf Head River.

Seven soldiers and the two surveyors had gone down to the creek to water the horses while, as per Fargo's orders, two privates kept watch from the butte tops. It appeared now, as two more soldiers were shot from their mounts and an Indian knelt beside a wounded surveyor, wielding a knife with which he no doubt intended to relieve the man of his hair, that none were coming back.

A spine-jellying scream rose from below. Fargo looked into the canyon. A brave stood over Valeria Howard, leaning down to smash the back of his right hand across the girl's face with a resounding smack. He pulled her up brusquely and, using both hands, ripped her shirtwaist down the front then threw his head back to loose a delighted whoop toward the sky.

Fargo raised the .44, but he couldn't see clearly over the stage roof.

He holstered the Colt and scrambled back along the rock wall. Dropping onto the stage, he raked the .44 from its holster. Off the coach's south side, the Indian had crouched to fling the major's daughter over his back like a sack of parched corn.

Naked to her waist, the blouse hanging in tatters around her thighs, the girl kicked, screamed, and pounded her fist into the brave's broad back. As the Indian turned to run off with his prize, Fargo steadied the pistol, angling it down from his right shoulder, and squeezed the trigger.

4

The Colt roared and leaped in his hand. The bullet ripped through the back of the Indian's head and careened out his forehead with a small geyser of bone, brains, and blood.

Valeria screamed as though she herself had been shot. The Indian ran several more feet toward the gap in the canyon wall, knees bending as the life drained out of him. He fell in a rolling, tumbling heap, the girl rolling through the dust and sage ahead of him, skirts and torn shirtwaist flopping around her hips.

She'd barely stopped rolling when Fargo, having leaped down from the stage and sprinted past the quivering Indian, pulled her brusquely to her feet, her breasts jiggling, red hair falling across her face and dusty, porcelain shoulders.

"Noooo!" she cried, shaking her head wildly and beating her fists against his shoulders.

"Keep your pants on—it's me!" he yelled as he wrapped his left arm around her waist and half dragged, half carried her toward his Ovaro stallion tied behind the stagecoach.

In the south, the Indians' whoops and shouts grew louder, hooves thumping, guns popping. Evidently, a couple of soldiers were putting up a fight, but they couldn't keep it up for long. He'd seen close to twenty braves along the creek, and judging by the sound of approaching horses, they were headed toward the coach.

"Where . . . what . . . ?" the girl gasped as Fargo holstered his Colt, wrapped his hands around her waist, and tossed her onto the pinto's back. The horse was skitter-stepping at the gunfire, twitching its ears and snorting.

Fargo ripped the reins from the stage's luggage boot, then shucked his Henry repeater from the sheath attached to the saddle. "We're gonna haul ass outta

5

here!" He swung up behind the girl. She halfheartedly crossed her arms over her breasts and looked around, sobbing.

As the Trailsman reined the pinto away from the stage, an arrow whistled through the air behind his head and clattered into the canyon wall to his right. He swung a look left as two painted braves clad only in loincloths, moccasins, and war paint galloped their paint ponies through the notch in the canyon wall, screaming like devils loosed from hell. Their medicine pouches and bone necklaces jostled wildly.

As one jerked his mount to a skidding halt and reached into his quiver for another arrow, the other flung a war hatchet. Fargo reined the pinto toward the two braves as the hatchet careened wickedly past his left cheek to bury its head in the stage's thin housing.

The Trailsman snapped the Henry to his shoulder and fired two quick shots, firing and cocking and firing again. Hearing the braves scream but not waiting around to watch them fly off their horses, the Trailsman reined the Ovaro out ahead of the stage and gouged the stallion's flanks with his spurs.

"Keep your head down!" he ordered the girl as several arrows and bullets careened through the air around them, plunking into the dust on both sides of the two-track trail.

Fargo took his rifle in his right hand, reins in the left, then snaked that arm around the girl's waist, drawing her taut against him.

The Ovaro lowered its own head and, snorting, mane buffeting, lunged down the trail in a ground-eating gallop. This wasn't the stallion's first encounter with Indians, and the smell of blood and bear grease and the savage, elemental sound of the whoops and yowls and the creaking twang of bows and arrows chilled his blood and rendered his hooves light as feathers.

"What about the soldiers?" the girl cried above the thunder of the pinto's hooves.

"Finished!" Fargo shouted, turning in his saddle to fire his Henry repeater one-handed behind him at the six or seven braves giving chase, hunkered low over the necks of their lunging ponies.

"What about my luggage?" she cried. "All my belongings are on the *stage!*"

Two arrows thumped into the ground on both sides of the trail. Several slugs sliced the air over Fargo's head, one ricocheting loudly off a rock.

"If you want to go back for it, you're on your own!" Fargo shouted, loosing another shot behind.

"But . . . but . . . I have nothing to *wear!*"

Fargo jerked a look behind and shook the Ovaro's reins, urging more speed. "If we don't lose these savages, you won't *need* anything!"

As rifles popped behind him, he leaned forward to yell in the horse's ear. "Come on, boy! Split the trail *wide open!*"

The girl jerked her head toward the Trailsman accusingly, brows furrowed, lips parted, fire red hair jostling across her eyes. Fargo was about to ask what the look was about, but then he realized his left arm was pushing up beneath her naked breasts.

He gave a sheepish half smile, loosened his grip, then turned to fling another shot behind them.

2

The Ovaro was not only the fastest horse Fargo had ever ridden, but it had plenty of bottom, too. More bottom than the Indians' mustangs, obviously, because Fargo and Valeria Howard gradually pulled away from their pursuers, until the braves' gunshots sounded little louder than snapping twigs, and the thunder of their ponies was like the distant passing of a fleeting summer storm.

When they'd ridden a good four miles beyond the scene of the attack, Fargo pulled the horse off the old traders' trail he'd been following, and into a cut between high, chalky buttes. A light breeze rose, and the Ovaro lifted its head, sniffing and softly nickering. Fargo turned the horse to look behind, tipping his hat against the sun.

About a half mile straight east of the traders' trail, six or seven Indians were walking their horses along the base of a jog of curving hogbacks, riding slowly away from Fargo and Valeria. Their leader wore a buffalo headdress. They were armed with either bows and arrows or carbines. Hatchets swung from their belts. A couple of the young braves held war lances adorned with tribal feathers.

Judging by the tribal feathers and designs painted on their faces and horses, these braves were Assiniboine, not Blackfeet, like those behind Fargo.

Valeria Howard shivered on the saddle before the Trailsman. "Oh, God . . ."

Fargo studied the riders until they'd disappeared down the other side of a distant slope. *Oh, God* was right. They were surrounded by Indians.

Fargo turned the Ovaro and galloped west between the buttes.

"Where are we going?" the girl asked, craning her neck to peer over Fargo's shoulder.

"The pinto needs water. There's a spring around here." Fargo glanced behind, and seeing no redskins on his trail, checked the sweat-lathered Ovaro down to a walk. "About two prairie swells farther west is a trading post and stage station. We'll stop there for the night."

Crossing her bare arms over her pale breasts, the girl looked up at him. Her face was dust streaked, and weed seeds clung to her mussed, russet-colored hair. There was a fearful trill in her voice. "But we could make Fort Clark in a couple of hours!"

"If we kept moving as fast as we've *been* moving, we could make the fort about three hours after good dark. But the horse is tired. And we don't want to be out here after dark."

Valeria looked around warily, at the eroded butte faces and breeze-ruffled buffalo grass, at the dry, chalky wash meandering through the gray-brown grass tall enough to conceal a crawling Indian. "Father is going to be worried." She swung her gaze back to Fargo, eyes sharp. "How could you let this happen? You were supposed to be *watching* for Indians! That's why Father *hired* you!"

"You're alive, aren't you? Still have your topknot."

Fargo reined the horse into a hollow at the base of a high butte. Water bubbled up from the butte's base, around sand and mossy, pitted boulders, and emanated a vague sulfur smell. Cattails grew along the spring's perimeter, and meadowlarks rode the swaying weed tips, a few lighting as the Ovaro drew up and Fargo slipped off the horse's back.

He dropped the pinto's reins and reached up to help the girl down. She'd forgotten to cover her breasts as she stared into the distance, her face drawn with worry. Fargo couldn't help letting his gaze linger over the softly rounded, pink-tipped orbs, no less enticing for being rimed with trail dust and belonging to a rather haughty debutante.

She glanced down at him, saw where his eyes were, and gasped. Quickly, she drew the frayed strips of her torn blouse closed. "Isn't there something besides staring at my breasts you should be doing, Mr. Fargo? Perhaps making sure we're not attacked *again* by those *savages*!"

Fargo wrapped his hand around her waist and pulled her roughly out of the saddle, evoking another gasp.

"I reckon," he said, setting her on the ground, glancing again at the pale orbs peeking out between the insufficient flaps of cloth. She smelled sweet, like talcum and lilacs, in spite of the ordeal. "But it won't be near as much fun."

He opened one of his saddlebags and rummaged around before pulling out a shirt sewn from flannel trade cloth, with badger teeth for buttons. He tossed the shirt to the girl. "Why don't you put that on so I can concentrate on my job?"

"Oh, I suppose the Indians surprised you because of *me*!" she said, turning her back and flapping out the overlarge shirt in front of her.

Fargo grabbed his spyglass out of his saddlebags and began climbing the slope rising east of the spring.

The girl called behind him, "You don't have something a little smaller?"

Halfway up the slope, Fargo stopped and turned toward her. She remained standing with her naked back to him, holding the shirt up to inspect it.

"I wasn't packing for you!" As he continued climbing, he glanced over his shoulder and said quietly, "Get a drink. We'll be movin' out in two minutes."

"Uncouth bastard," she grumbled behind him.

Fargo dropped down against the bluff, doffed his hat, and telescoped the spyglass. He'd no sooner trained the glass on their back trail between the two ridges than his back tensed and his gut filled with bile.

Shadows of galloping riders undulated across the grassy southern slopes of the shallow canyon. A few beats later, the Indians he'd spied a little while earlier appeared around a bend, the brave in the buffalo headdress riding point, batting his moccasined heels against the ribs of his chuffing, galloping paint.

Behind Fargo, the Ovaro snorted loudly. Down the canyon galloping hooves rumbled.

"What's the matter with—?" The girl stopped as Fargo slammed the end of the spyglass against his palm, reducing it, then grabbed his hat and began scrambling down the slope, leaping rocks and tufts of sage and silverthorn.

"Mount up!"

"What is it?"

Fargo hit the bottom of the canyon running, grabbed the girl around the waist, and heaved her back onto the pinto. "Mount *up*!"

He grabbed the reins, tossed the spyglass into the saddlebags, then leaped up behind the girl who jerked her head around, whimpering, as the thud of hooves rose from down the canyon.

"Hold on!"

Fargo reined the horse away from the spring and into the crease. Immediately, shrill whoops and yowls rose on his left, above the thuds of the pounding hooves.

Fargo turned the pinto westward along the crease, then gave the horse its head. The Ovaro stretched out, bounding through the hock-high grass as the Indians' enraged whoops and yowls grew behind it, the cacophony punctuated by sporadic gunfire.

"How did they *find* us?" the girl cried, the tails of the long shirt whipping out around her.

"The breeze switched." Fargo glanced back to see the half dozen Indians bolting toward them, the broad chests of their paints and pintos and Appaloosas glistening in the afternoon sunlight, the braves' yells echoing around the buttes. "They must've smelled your perfume."

"Why didn't you . . . ?"

"Sorry, honey," Fargo growled. "I can't control the wind!"

He glanced behind once more. Whooping like a crazed warlock, the lead warrior held up a feathered war lance dyed red, green, and black, his medicine pouch and necklaces dancing along his broad, muscular chest. The brave's right cheek appeared covered with a strawberry birthmark beneath the swirling lines of war paint.

"That looks like the son of Iron Shirt," Fargo muttered darkly as he turned forward, flinching at an arrow sailing across his left shoulder.

Arrows sliced the air above and around them, and a rifle barked, a slug spanging off a rock only a few feet right of the galloping pinto. Ahead, the crease

12

between the buttes curved right, then narrowed to a couple of yards.

"Take the reins!" Fargo yelled above the thunder of the Ovaro's slicing, grinding hooves, shoving the ribbons into the girl's hands.

Valeria shot him a wary glance.

"Keep riding. When you clear these buttes, stop and wait for me atop that flat-topped bluff in the distance."

Stiffly, her cheeks pale with terror, the girl took the reins reluctantly, as though they were on fire, and stared warily down at the lunging horse. "What're you going to *do*?"

Fargo shucked his Henry rifle, cocked it one-handed. "I'm gonna clean those wolves off our trail!"

Throwing both arms out for balance, Fargo hopped straight back along the horse's rocking hips.

He glanced behind. The Indians were out of sight beyond the bend in the crease, but they wouldn't be for long.

Fargo threw himself straight back off the Ovaro's rump, hitting the ground flat-footed. Propelled by the horse's momentum, he rolled through the grass, managing to hold on to the rifle. As he began to slow, his right knee nipped a rock along the trail, and he gritted his teeth.

Cursing, he rolled off his shoulder and shot a look up the trail. The horse and the girl galloped away from him, the girl glancing over her shoulder, red hair bouncing along her back.

Fargo waved her on, then threw himself off the trail. As the whoops and hooffalls grew louder behind him, he scrambled up the steeply shelving butte on his left.

He doffed his hat and lifted a look over the butte's shoulder. At the same time, the Indian with the head-dress and birthmark—Iron Shirt's oldest son, sure enough—dashed around the bend on his fleet-footed paint, the other five howling braves pushing in close around him so all six could squeeze through the narrow corridor.

The Trailsman pushed himself straight up to the crest of the butte shoulder and, on one knee, snapped the Henry to his cheek. Iron Shirt's son—Blaze Face—glanced up as his paint approached the gap before him.

The warrior's spotted face blanched and his lower jaw dropped a half second before Fargo blew him out of his saddle, sending the headdress flying. Fargo jacked another round into the chamber and fired, and continued firing until all six horses were galloping through the gap without riders, or, as in the case of a small-boned Appy, kicking its rider along under its scissoring hooves.

As gun smoke billowed around Fargo's head, he turned to look up trail. The last rider rolled through the crease and piled up against a boulder.

Fargo scrambled down the butte and ran up to the warrior, who lay against the boulder spotted with the young man's blood. Several broken ribs poked through his bloody sides. The brave kicked miserably, arching his back and groaning.

The Trailsman racked a fresh shell into the Henry's breech and held the barrel two inches from the brave's right eye. "Why are you raiding?" he demanded in Sioux, hoping he had the right dialect.

The brave shook the hair from his eyes and spat several curses which, in good Indian style, insulted not only the Trailsman's mother and sisters but his female cousins, as well. The brave had opened his mouth to launch another tirade, when he tensed suddenly.

Apparently, one of the broken ribs had pierced his heart. He flung his head back with an audible smack against the ground, gave another couple of kicks, and lay still, eyes glazed with death.

The Trailsman cursed in the Indian's tongue, then, knowing the gunfire might have been heard by other warriors, turned away from the dead brave and jogged up the trail, thumbing fresh shells from his cartridge belt into the Henry's loading tube.

He hadn't walked far before the girl and the pinto rose up from behind a grassy, breeze-brushed knoll. The pinto snorted and trotted forward, nearly running Fargo over before swerving sideways, stopping, snorting again, and shaking its glistening black mane, relieved to find that the Trailsman had survived the Indians. The golden late-afternoon sunshine made the strip of white between the horse's fore- and hindquarters glow. It made the girl's red hair shimmer like sunset hues reflected off a high mountain lake.

"I thought I told you to wait on that bluff yonder," Fargo snapped at her, sliding his Henry into the saddle sheath.

She stared down at him, glowing red hair dancing around her head. "I was worried about you."

"Well, don't be," Fargo snapped, grabbing the reins out of her hands and swinging up into the saddle. "Just do what I tell you!"

"Fine, then," she said, crossing her arms over her chest, the overlarge tunic billowing out around them. "Just *fine*!"

Fargo turned the pinto around, heeled it west. The girl, nearly tossed from the saddle as the horse leaped forward, gave a startled cry and lunged for the horn.

3

When Fargo and Valeria Howard had ridden for another twenty minutes, it wasn't more Indians they found themselves shadowed by, but a mass of swollen purple clouds driven toward them by a knife-edged wind.

The prairie hogbacks turned lemon yellow. Thunder rumbled and lightning flashed. The sudden gale shepherded tumbleweeds across the short brown grass and thrashed the scattered cottonwoods and oaks. Prairie dogs squealed and ran for their burrows.

"Shit!" Fargo said, turning his head forward and tipping his hat brim low.

Ahead, he could make out the brown smudge of the old trading post nestled between hogbacks about a half mile away, smoke skeining from its large fieldstone chimney.

"Hold on!" he yelled above the howling wind and rumbling thunder, clucking the Ovaro into another ground-eating lope.

They hadn't galloped thirty yards before the storm converged on them, rain pouring out of the dark clouds, driven slantwise by the wind. Fargo and the girl hunkered low in the saddle as the Ovaro galloped over one rise and down another, hooves splashing through puddles, the wind-whipped rain pummeling the Trailsman's shoulders and pasting his buckskin tunic against his back and sluicing off the broad brim of his high-crowned hat.

As they galloped over the last rise, the trading post/ stage station appeared before them, nestled in a broad hollow and fronted by a creek sheathed in cattails. It was a broad, tall, barnlike building of stout logs with a low, brush-roofed stable attached to the side. The post's windows were shuttered, and the stable doors were closed, but wan lamplight seeped out through gaps between the logs and through the rifle slits in the front doors and shutters.

Lightning flashed and thunder clapped as the Ovaro splashed across the creek, which broiled with muddy, fast-moving water, and lunged up the opposite bank. It galloped past the stone well house and into the yard that had become a rain-pelted slough, and skidded to a slipping, sliding halt before the stable.

Three tarp-covered freight wagons sat nearby, wagon tongues drooping, the tarp groaning and flapping in the wind.

Fargo slipped out of the pinto's saddle, lost his footing in the soggy mud, and nearly fell before regaining his balance and drawing the stable doors open. He led the pinto into the stable's murky, musty shadows rife with the smell of hay and ammonia. A couple of horses, hidden in the shadows, loosed frightened whinnies and kicked their stall partitions, frightened by the storm as well as the intruders. In the stable's far recesses, a cat growled angrily.

Fargo lifted Valeria Howard out of the saddle. Soaked, she weighed a good ten pounds more than she had when he'd put her there. Her red hair hung straight down her back, and she crossed her arms and hunched her shoulders, shivering.

"I'll get you into the lodge!" he yelled above the wind pummeling the doors and stout log walls, making the rafters creak. He ran his hand down the pinto's sleek, wet neck. "You stay, boy. I'll be back to bed you down."

He ushered her through the stable doors, led her by the hand along the front of the stable to the porch. She gave a cry as water streamed off the sagging porch roof and down her back.

"Could I be any more miserable?" she said, shivering, hugging herself, as Fargo led her up the porch steps.

He rapped on the stout log door. Almost immediately, a rifle barrel pushed through one of the two slots in the door's vertical half logs. Behind the door, a man's voice squawked, "Friend or foe, red man or white?"

Fargo glanced at the round musket barrel sliding around in the slot, and at the rheumy blue eye peeking out the hole from inside.

"It's Skye Fargo, Smiley. Open up!"

The musket barrel wobbled around, twitched, and receded into the cabin. A thump sounded from inside, followed by the scrape of a locking bar. The door opened a foot, and a round, bald head poked out, blue eyes wide with caution. When the eyes found Fargo, the old man's lower jaw dropped.

"Skye Fargo! Well, I'll be skinned! Get on in here outta the damp, ya crazy coon!"

The old man threw the door wide and stepped back inside the cabin. Fargo followed him in, drawing the girl along behind him.

Old Smiley Bristo stood just inside the door, flexing

his snakeskin spats and grinning broadly, toothlessly up at the Trailsman towering over him. His breath was fetid with yeasty beer, whiskey, and tobacco. "What the hell brings you up to this country, Skye? How long's it been, anyways . . . ?"

The old man's voice trailed off as his drink-bleary gaze slid to the girl stepping up beside Fargo. "Well, I'll be hanged," he said, voiced hushed with awe, raking an index finger through his silvery patch beard. "You got a *woman* with ya."

The word "woman" had no sooner escaped the oldster's lips than the half dozen men sitting at the tables in the room's smoky shadows, right of the long plank bar running along the room's left wall, swiveled toward Fargo and the girl. The Trailsman's eyes had not yet adjusted to the room's shadows, which were shunted to and fro by hanging oil lamps and the cracking fire in the giant fieldstone hearth. But one look at the shirt clinging like a second skin to Valeria's full breasts, nipples jutting from behind the soaked wool, told him what their eyes had found.

Valeria, apparently, had also become aware of the men's scrutiny. Shyly, she turned her back to the men, and cast Fargo an uneasy sidelong glance.

"The lady would like a room and a hot bath," Fargo said. "Some dry clothes, if you got any."

His eyes glued to the girl, Smiley opened his mouth to speak, but stopped when a low voice rumbled from a table near the fire. "Shee-it, she need her back washed, too?"

Chuckles washed up from the webbing smoke and jostling shadows, heads jerking.

The girl sidled up close to Fargo as the old man said, his voice hushed as before, "I usually give the ladies from the stage the Chicago room upstairs, between New York and Abilene, as the curtains is pink and the mattress is goose feathers, plucked and stuffed myself. I'll heat some water pronto. And I'll rustle up a shirt and britches though I don't have much in the way of female frillies." He glanced shyly at the girl with a truckling bow. "Are you hungry, miss? I got a nice stew on the fire—the kidneys of a sow griz I just shot yesterday. The boys has already had some, and nobody's been sick so far!"

Valeria splayed her hand on her chest and cleared her throat. "The food sounds delightful, but I think just the room and the bath will do for now."

"I'll show the lady to her room, Smiley," Fargo said, taking the girl's arm, "if you wanna get started on the water."

When the old man nodded and turned toward the curtained door behind the bar, Fargo began leading the girl toward the stairs at the back of the room. The girl stopped and turned toward the old man. "Oh, Mr. . . . uh . . . Smiley," she said haltingly. "I was wondering if there was . . . a . . . *lock* on the door?"

Again, snickers and chuckles rose from amongst the tables, chairs creaking.

Smiley turned at the curtained doorway, frowning as though he wasn't sure he understood. "Why . . . no, ma'am. No locks. Never seen no need for none."

Fargo forced a smile and continued leading the girl between the bar and the tables. As he walked, his eyes adjusted well enough that he could make out a few of the bearded faces turned toward them, recognizing a couple of burly mule skinners from Canada and a gambler from Council Bluffs.

At the back of the room, he and Valeria mounted the creaky stairs. He glanced over his shoulder to make sure none of the men, still staring after them, was leveling a gun at him or preparing to toss a knife at his back. At the top of the stairs, he loosed a relieved breath and led Valeria along the dim hall, the girl starting at the thunder cracking outside and making dust sift from the rafters.

All the doors bore wooden plaques into which the names of American cities had been burned, most misspelled. He stopped before the one labeled CHIKAGO, and threw it open.

"Home sweet home," Fargo said, turning away.

She grabbed his arm. "You're not going to leave me alone, are you?"

Fargo dropped his eyes to her shirt. "You want me to stay and help you out of your wet duds?"

"Don't be ridiculous!" she snapped, balling the front of the dripping shirt in her fist, the shirt making a slight sucking sound as she pulled it away from her skin. She glanced down the dim hall, lightning flashing in the room's single window, thunder shaking the floor and rattling a picture hanging on the wall near the door. "You saw the way those men were staring at me."

"Can't say as I blame 'em." The Trailsman peeled the girl's hand off his arm and started down the hall. "I'll be back as soon as I've tended my horse and grabbed a bottle."

"Mr. Fargo?" she said, her voice trembling.

With a sigh, he turned back to her once more.

She moved toward him, placed her hands on his arms as she stared up with beseeching eyes, digging her fingers into his biceps. "I'm frightened. I know it's not proper but . . . will you stay with me tonight? In . . . my room, I mean."

Fargo grinned down at her.

She frowned indignantly, dropped her hands, and put a little steel into her quivering voice. "You can stop smiling. I am certainly not inviting you into my bed, sir!"

Fargo wrapped his arms around her waist and drew him to her brusquely. She gasped as he lowered his head and closed his mouth over hers. At first, she was as stiff as a fence post in his arms, but in seconds she began to soften. He probed her upper lip with his tongue, slipped it inside her mouth. Immediately, as though catching herself, she gave an angry grunt, placed her hands against his chest, and pushed away from him.

Her chest heaving, she scowled up at him, and slapped him hard across the face.

He smiled, drew her to him once more. Again she gasped as he pressed his lips to hers. This time, she didn't fight him.

When he pulled away, she stared up at him, her eyes soft, lips parted, the clinging shirt outlining each full breast clearly as she threw her shoulders back, the beautiful orbs rising and falling like barrels on a storm-tossed sea.

"We'll discuss the sleeping arrangements later," Fargo said. "Now, if you'll excuse me, I'll see to my horse."

As he stepped back away from her, she stumbled toward him, regained her balance, and stared up at him, wide green eyes like two glowing agates in the shadows. His pants feeling frustratingly tight, Fargo tipped his soggy hat to her, turned away, and tramped off down the hall. He could feel the girl's eyes branding his back until he turned and descended the stairs, boots clomping on the scarred cottonwood planks, spurs chinging, the storm booming around him, rain pelting the roof.

The room hushed as Fargo crossed the main hall toward the bar, heads turning to stare at him from the smoky shadows. The air was so thick with the smell

22

of leather, cigarette and wood smoke, and the spicy aromas of the bear kidney stew that there seemed hardly any oxygen.

Smiley stood at the bar, laying out a game of solitaire, a half-filled beer mug near his left arm. He looked up as the Trailsman approached.

"I'm heating water for the girl's bath. You look like you could use a drink."

"Whiskey," Fargo said. "Give me the stuff without the snake venom."

"Shit," Smiley chuckled, reaching under the bar and setting a brown bottle onto the planks. "It's *all* snake venom, Skye. You been through here enough times to know that!"

The oldster grabbed a shot glass off a nearby pyramid, popped the bottle's cork, and splashed the murky brown fluid into the glass. "Where did you find little miss, if you don't mind me askin'. I been in these parts long enough to know she didn't come from any of the settlements around here."

"Major Howard's daughter." The Trailsman sipped the whiskey. It did indeed taste like snake venom with two parts gunpowder to one part coal oil and a whole lot of chili pepper. When it had scraped about all the skin from his throat it was going to, he held the glass up to look at it. "I and about nine soldiers were takin' her to Fort Clark when Blackfeet attacked. Wiped out the whole party except me and her."

"The Blackfeet been on the prod of late."

Fargo glanced up at the old man leaning toward him on his elbows. "Them and the Assiniboine?"

"Sure as smelly water in a whore's boudoir." Smiley pronounced that last "boydee-are." He shook his grizzled head and took a swig of beer. "You'd swear they all be usin' prickly pears to wipe their asses. They took out three cabins just north of here, a ranch out west, and a tradin' post up on the south fork of Misery Creek."

He nodded at the two burly, buckskin-clad men playing poker in front of the fire, both with fat stogies wedged in their mouths. "The mule skinners said a howlin' group of the red-niggers done burned one of them new settlements on the Cannonball!"

Fargo didn't like the debris floating around inside his whiskey glass, but he'd tasted worse and it was tempering the chill in his bones. "They leave you alone?"

"Hell, they don't come near me," Smiley said, re-filling Fargo's glass. "This place is stout as a stockade. Besides, they like my hooch and trade cloth."

Fargo reached for his refilled glass. A hide pouch flew over his left shoulder and clattered onto the bar planks before him. A couple of gold coins dribbled out of the neck onto the bar.

The Trailsman turned slowly toward the room. One of the mule skinners, Pierre Bardot, stood with one stovepipe boot perched on his chair. He was a couple of inches taller than the Trailsman, which put him close to seven feet. He wore a black sombrero thronged beneath his chin, curly red hair tufting out around it. His tattooed arms were thick as fence posts, his red-brown eyes small as trade beads.

"For the woman," said Bardot in his faint French accent, giving a self-important nod.

The mule skinner's partner, a Scandinavian named Hallbing—a one-eyed blond with a knife scar along his bearded right cheek—lounged back in his chair, one brawny arm draped over the chair back. He grinned at Fargo, showing his small, cracked, tobacco-stained teeth, his lone eye narrowed.

Lightning flashed in the windows. Thunder rocked the room.

Fargo glanced at the gold coins, turned back to the man who'd tossed the pouch. "Don't tempt me," he drawled, turning back toward his glass.

Something whistled through the air over Fargo's right shoulder. The rusty-bladed, bone-handled knife plunked into the bar planks before the money sack, six inches from Fargo's left hand. The vibrating handle sang like a mouth harp.

When the song faded, the mule skinner's voice rumbled like thunder in Fargo's ear. "Take it or leave it."

4

Glancing at the knife embedded in the bar planks, Fargo again turned to face the room. The French-Canadian mule skinner, Bardot, strolled toward him, big boots clomping along the roadhouse's puncheons. His sombrero shaded his face, but as he approached the bar, a lamp found the tiny, steely eyes set deep in the man's doughy, red-bearded face.

He grinned, showing a wide gap where his two front teeth should have been. He spoke slowly, loudly, each word spat out in the freighter's French accent. "I said take it or leave it, friend."

Fargo smiled amiably and poked his soaked hat off his forehead. "She's not for sale, friend."

"No, no, no," the big freighter said, shaking his head and frowning. "She *is* for sale, and you can either take the money or leave it. Either way, the girl is mine tonight, and she goes with me and my partner *tomorrow*."

He grinned, but his tiny eyes were hard.

Fargo maintained his affable smile. "You're just not gonna take no for an answer, are you, friend?"

The freighter continued grinning at him.

Keeping his eyes on the big man before him, Fargo

reached back, plucked the coin pouch off the bar, and thrust it against the man's chest, the coins clinking around inside.

The freighter dropped his gaze to the pouch, returned it to Fargo.

The Trailsman held the man's hard glare.

The freighter lurched forward, red-faced, swinging his ham-sized right fist toward Fargo's face.

The Trailsman, anticipating the punch, grabbed the man's wrist and, pivoting, bulled the man's back against the bar and thrust the man's hand out across the planks. Pressing his own back against the man's chest, wedging him against the bar, Fargo reached out with his free hand, plucked the knife from the bar top, and slammed it through the freighter's open palm and into the wood.

"Uhhhh!" the man bellowed like a bull in an abattoir, turning his head toward his hand from which his own knife protruded, pinned to the rough-hewn planks.

Bright red blood welled up around the rusty blade.

Fargo heard a chair rake across the room's puncheons and saw the Norwegian bound up out of his seat, reaching for one of his two holstered six-shooters positioned for the cross draw. The Trailsman palmed his own Colt .44, clicked the hammer back, aiming from his belly.

The big Norski froze. Around him, the other four men had fallen silent, still seated at their tables, sliding their cautious gazes between the big Norwegian, the Frenchman who was still pinned to the bar with his own knife, and Fargo.

The Norski freighter stumbled back drunkenly, then, letting his hand fall away from his holster, sagged down in his chair.

Fargo glanced at the Frenchman. The man had

drawn his other hand cautiously up to the bar. Now he wrapped it around the knife handle and, stretching his lips back from his empty, tobacco-dark gums, gave a hoarse grunt as he pulled the knife out of the bar.

Clutching the bloody appendage to his chest, he dropped to the floor, wincing and cursing and glaring up at Fargo.

The Trailsman holstered his Colt, turned to the bar, and threw back his second whiskey shot. Setting the glass back onto the bar, he glanced at Smiley, who was scrubbing at the bloody planks with a damp cloth, as though blood were spilled there all the time.

"I'm gonna see to my horse," Fargo said above another thunderclap, pulling his hat brim down over his eyes. "Make sure no one goes upstairs, will you?"

"That includin' me? I hear the water boilin' for the lady's bath."

"You can go. Take her some food, too," Fargo said, reaching for the door handle. He glanced back at the old barkeep, curling his lip wryly. "But keep it in your pants."

With that he glanced once more at the redheaded Frenchman sitting with his back against a beer keg holding up the bar planks, still grunting and cursing and glaring at Fargo as he wrapped a blue bandanna around his shaking, bloody hand.

Fargo tipped his hat to the man, opened the door, went out, and closed the door behind him. He stepped to the edge of the porch.

The rain was only dribbling off the porch roof now. The thunder rumbled off in the distance. A forked lightning bolt flashed over a distant knoll to the north, but another mass of purple clouds was moving in from the east.

The bad weather wasn't over yet. That was all right

with Fargo. He didn't doubt the Indians valued Smiley's hooch too much to attack the outpost, but he favored the reassurance of the storm.

A bunch of braves mixing from two separate tribes, broiling with fury and sharpening their horns for the white-eyes, tended to cut a broad swath.

Fargo stepped off the porch and slogged through the mud and lightly pelting rain to the stable. When he'd unleathered the Ovaro, stabled him, rubbed him down with dry burlap, and fed and watered him, he headed back outside, his rifle in his right hand, saddlebags and bedroll draped over his right shoulder.

The sun had gone down and the eastern storm chugged and flashed over the southeastern hills, but there was a lull in the rain. The air was fragrant with the smell of damp earth, sage, and brimstone.

After a cursory inspection of the grounds around the trading post and finding no sign of prowling redskins, the Trailsman walked back around to the front of the roadhouse and, resting one hand on his pistol grips, pushed through the door.

Inside the lodge, he'd half expected to see a knife thrown toward him, or a pistol aimed his way. Instead, as he blinked through the smoky shadows as though through layers of dirty gauze, he found two men—drovers, judging by their batwing chaps and sun-seared faces—dancing hand in hand and grinning from ear to ear.

One of the others sang softly of Dakota sunsets, of ancient Indians hunting buffalo, and of walking arm in arm along a creek with a girl named Rose.

The big Norwegian sat passed out in his chair, head on the table before him. The redheaded freighter, Bardot, sat with his back against the wall beside the snapping hearth, cradling his wounded appendage in his lap like a pet. In his other hand, he held an uncorked bottle. The light was too dim for Fargo to be sure, but the man's eyes appeared open, his face expressionless.

Good and soused. Too soused to make trouble, Fargo hoped.

He removed his hand from his pistol grips, closed the door, and stepped into the room. He'd taken two steps before a French-accented voice rumbled softly from across the room, "This ain't over, Fargo." The Frenchman held up his injured hand, and winced. "Ain't over by a long shot!"

Boots thumped on the stairs, and Fargo turned to see Smiley descending from the second-story shadows, swinging an empty bucket in each hand. "Filled the lady's tub," the oldster said, grinning lasciviously. "Most fun I had in a month of Sundays!"

"You need to get out more, Smiley," Fargo said, pouring a fresh drink from the bottle on the bar.

Smiley set the buckets down and grabbed a wooden bowl heaped with steaming kidney stew off the bar's far end. "I'll bring her some of my good griz kidney to eat with her bath!"

As the old man wheeled toward the stairs, Fargo tossed the empty glass on the bar, and grabbed the bottle by its neck. "You've done enough, Smiley." He strolled down the bar and took the bowl from the oldster's hands. "Let me give you a hand."

"Ah, have a heart, Skye!" the old man complained as Fargo climbed the stairs.

Fargo strode down the hall to the Chicago room, boots clomping, spurs chinking. Rain tattooed the roof and lightning flashed between the logs at the end of the hall where the chinking had crumbled.

He tripped the lever latch and pushed the pine-plank door open with one hand. Standing in the steaming copper tub and running the soap across her breasts, the girl turned toward him and gasped. She allowed him a lingering peek at her sudsy, pale breasts before she raised an arm, feigning outrage.

"Can't you *knock*?"

Fargo stepped into the room and kicked the door closed, running his eyes across the girl's incredible figure—long-limbed, pale, full-busted, and round-hipped. She'd pinned her damp hair atop her head, and several wisps curled down around her sculpted cheeks.

"You heard me comin'," Fargo said knowingly, keeping his eyes on her as he set the bottle and the bowl on the dresser.

Suds moved in miniature glaciers down her arms and thighs, winking in the wan lantern light. She narrowed her eyes accusingly. "What're you *saying*?"

Fargo took a long pull from the bottle then threw his hat on a chair. Unbuttoning his wet shirt, he turned toward Valeria Howard, regarding her coolly, with open appraisal, as he shrugged out of the shirt and threw it onto the floor near the small, cast-iron wood stove in the corner.

She said nothing but only let her eyes flick across his broad chest and muscular arms as he peeled the wet underwear top off his shoulders, then kicked out of his boots and unbuttoned his buckskin breeches.

As he kicked out of the breeches and long underwear bottoms, and stepped toward her naked, her gaze dropped to his jutting member. Her green eyes flickered. A deep flush rose from nearly as far down as her breasts to spread into her cheeks and temples.

Her eyes stayed on his shaft until, grabbing the soap out of her hand, he stepped around behind her, slid his arms under hers, took the soap-slick orbs in his hands, and began to gently massage them, running the soap cake over each.

As he did, she threw her head back, sighing. "Father would have you shot for this," she breathed, pressing her lips against his shoulder.

Fargo continued working the soap into her breasts, lowering his hands occasionally to caress her taut, smooth belly, dipping as far down as her love nest to evoke a soft groan of pleasure. "And you?"

"And me?"

She placed a hand on his face, kissed him, nibbling his lips, then turned her body toward his, splashing water up around her knees in the copper tub.

"And me?"

It was barely a whisper this time as, slowly bending her knees and running her hands and lips down his body, she kissed his throat, chest, and belly. She cupped his balls in her slender hands, then slid her fingers up around the base of his bobbing member. Her breasts rising and falling heavily, she lowered her head to his shaft, closing her mouth over the engorged head.

A muscle twitched in Fargo's cheek as the hot moistness of her mouth slid gradually down his organ, her tongue flicking, caressing, probing, tickling.

When she'd taken as much of him as she could, she lifted coy green eyes to his, then slowly slid her lips back up toward the blood-engorged head. Fargo ground his feet into the puncheons and rested his hands in her hair.

She pulled her face away from his organ for just a moment, studying it dreamily, before lowering her head once again. She took him as far down as she could, then pulled back quickly, bathing nearly his entire length in hot saliva before lowering her head once more, faster this time . . . faster . . . until she was groaning, grunting, sighing as she ran her lips up and down his iron-hard shaft, head bobbing, her hands pumping when she wasn't sucking and running her lips around the head or down the side, flicking her ravenous, snakelike tongue.

"Christ . . ." Fargo groaned, fisting his hands in her hair, spreading his feet, and throwing his head back on his shoulders.

She half choked and groaned with excitement, her body tensing, cupping his balls in her hands as she worked even faster, harder.

When he was on the verge of explosion, he pushed her head away.

She groaned a protest, reaching for him.

"Time we did this good and proper," the Trailsman grunted.

Her wanton, little-girl eyes stayed with his rock-hard shaft as he lifted her up out of the tub, draped a towel around her shoulders, quickly dried her, then laid her back on the bed, displaying her before him like an exquisite, ivory-handled knife.

She groaned and panted like a she-lion, writhing around on the bed, reaching for him, spreading her legs and bending her knees, hair falling free from the makeshift knot atop her head.

"Hold on," he said, tossing the towel on the floor near the door, then retrieving his holstered Colt and cartridge belt.

"Skye!" she pleaded, reaching for his erection as he draped the belt around the bedpost nearest the door.

She twisted around on the bed, closing her fingers around his cock. He turned her onto her back as he knelt on the bed, then ran a hand between her spread legs, sliding his fingers through the silky, red down.

As wet as a cat in a rain barrel.

"Skye . . . !"

The Trailsman mounted her, slid his hands beneath her butt cheeks and pulled her up toward him as he

33

guided his shaft toward the glistening red fur between her legs.

"Ah, *Gawd*!" she cried as he slid inside, thrusting his powerful hips toward hers and spreading her knees like two halves of split birch.

They started off slowly, in and out, in and out, the bed creaking gently, the girl's spread legs bouncing, knees bending. After a couple of minutes, Fargo rose up on his arms and began increasing the beat, enjoying the sweet misery, the torture of holding himself back while the blood surged and raged in his loins.

He'd worked himself into a steady rhythm, when his keen ears detected a noise from the stairs.

He slowed the pace, lifted his head.

"No," she protested, placing her hands on his face and nibbling his lips hungrily. "Don't slow down . . . oh, *please*! . . . Don't slow down!"

Another sound rose from the stairs—the squawk of a loose step. Fargo continued thrusting. Valeria Howard groaned and shook her head like a mounted mare as the Trailsman regained his former rhythm, bucking against her wildly.

The girl sobbed and clawed at his shoulders, and the bed pitched like a rowboat on a storm-tossed sea.

Lightning flashed in the window. Rain tapped on the roof.

In the hall, a man laughed cunningly beneath the roar of a near thunderclap, and the thud of approaching boots grew and quickened—the stout, heavy-heeled boots of a mule skinner.

"Oh, Skye, oh, Skye!" Valeria Howard shrieked, digging her fingers into his shoulders and throwing her head back on the pillow.

Fargo gritted his teeth and dug his fingers into the corn-shuck mattress as he drove his ripe cock in and out of the girl's hot, sopping core. Beyond the door, the thunder of running boots stopped suddenly. A man's guffaw echoed around the hall.

"Skye, don't *stop!*" the girl shrieked.

Fargo continued thrusting and the girl continued groaning.

Thunder clapped and lightning flashed.

Supporting himself on his right arm, Fargo thrust his left hand at the bedpost, grabbed his Colt from his holster, and clicked the hammer back.

There was a huge explosion, as though the storm was suddenly inside the room. The door burst open to slam against the wall, slivers from the casing flying in all directions.

The French mule skinner's big frame filled the doorway, eyes glinting in the lamplight, frizzy red hair spilling down around his shoulders. Laughing wildly and shuttling his head from right to left, looking around the room, he swung his big six-shooter toward Fargo.

Fargo gave one final thrust between Valeria Howard's legs, and aimed the Colt at the doorway.

The forty-four roared and bucked in his hand. *Boom! Boom! Boom!*

Valeria Howard drove the back of her head into the pillow, arched her back, and howled as seed jettisoned from the Trailsman's heaving loins.

At the same time, the French freighter yowled like a lightning-struck bull and flew back out of the room and into the hall, triggering a bullet into the ceiling. He bounced off a wall and hit the floor, the report of his own impact and another thunderclap rocking the entire building.

"Oh, my God!" Valeria Howard bellowed, locking her ankles behind the Trailsman's back. *"Oh, my Gawwwwwwd!"*

5

When the smoke had cleared, Fargo shouted down the stairs for Smiley to cart the French trash out of the hall and to keep better tabs on his guests. Grumbling angrily, he rose naked from the bed, slammed the door, wedged a chair against it, and replaced the Colt's three spent shells with fresh ones.

Valeria Howard rose up on the bed, her hair in her eyes, looking shaken and disoriented. Feebly, she clutched a blanket to her breasts and stared at the door.

"What . . . ?"

"Nothing to worry about," the Trailsman said. "I think the frog eater was just inquiring the time."

Before she could form another question, Fargo climbed back onto the bed, gently pushed her down, turned her over, shoved her hair aside, and peppered her neck, back, and buttocks with kisses.

After the commotion in the hall had faded, the body hauled away, he quelled further questions by mounting her from behind—slow, easy, time-consuming strokes. If she remembered anything about the shooting, she mentioned nothing more about it for the rest of the storm- and love-tossed evening before she and

Fargo collapsed in each other's arms, her head on his chest, her hand proprietarily cupping his balls.

Fargo woke at the first wash of dawn and dressed quietly, letting Valeria sleep for a few more minutes, and went outside and scouted around before saddling the Ovaro and leading it back to the roadhouse. He woke the girl, and, sitting at a table downstairs, they enjoyed Smiley's breakfast of venison sausage and biscuits washed down with hot, black coffee.

All the men from the night before remained at the roadhouse—all except for the dead Frenchman, obviously, and his partner, Hallbing, who before dawn had headed out for Fort Clark with his wagonload of army supplies.

"Too bad Hallbing started out so early," Smiley said as Fargo scraped his chair back and tossed several coins on the table. "You three coulda ridden together. The Injuns leave that old Norski alone on account of he's married to a Sioux woman from over by Devils Lake and gives 'em free trade beads."

"I figured he might have been a little piss-burned over his partner," Fargo said, donning his hat as he ushered Valeria toward the door.

"Hallbing?"

Smiley laughed and followed Fargo and Valeria outside, where the air was cool and fresh after the storm, the yard pocked with mud puddles from which several sparrows and magpies bathed and drank. Meadowlarks piped on the dawn-washed prairie around the roadhouse.

"Hell, he's been wantin' to kill Bardot for a month of Sundays, on account of Bardot got one of Hallbing's daughters in the family way, if you'll pardon the expression, Miss Howard." The bearded oldster laughed again. "He just never had the guts to drop the hammer on him, I reckon. Besides, freightin' partners ain't all that easy to come by in these parts. If you see him," Smiley continued as Fargo swung up onto the Ovaro's back, "tell him he didn't leave enough lucre on the bar this mornin' to cover his bill. If he don't cough it up, his next time here he'll be drinkin' the snake venom I usually serve to the soldiers!"

Fargo reached down, took the girl's hand, and swung her up behind him. "How would he know the difference?" With that, he pinched his hat brim to Smiley, neck-reined the pinto around, and booted it into a trot across the muddy yard, heading southwest. Valeria sat behind him, her arms wrapped around his waist.

"Very funny, Fargo!" the roadhouse proprietor called, raising his voice as he added, "I reckon I'll dust off a bottle o' that coffin varnish for you, too!"

Fargo threw up an arm and put the Ovaro into a jog-trot, looking around carefully as the sun climbed toward the eastern horizon. Gray-purple shadows swelled out from buttes and hillocks and occasional cottonwood stands. The roadhouse was a good nine miles from Fort Clark—nine miles that at first gander appeared as open as a sea but were in fact scored with countless hidden coulees, ravines, and creek beds in which Indians might lie in ambush. The marauding redskins would most likely be holed up because of the rain, but leave it to an Indian to do the unexpected.

Fargo stayed clear of the wagon road connecting the roadhouse with Fort Clark, as the Indians were probably watching it. Traveling cross-country, he kept his eyes open, probing every rise and depression and every clump of bunchgrass and weed-choked boulder, ready to reach for his saddle gun.

Three miles from the roadhouse, and following a

well-worn but ancient Indian path, he drew rein in a ravine choked with wild rose and chokecherry shrubs. The ravine was probably dry most of the year, but last night's rain had sent water churning through it like whipped tea.

Keeping his eyes on the grassy rise south of the stream, Fargo slipped out of the saddle and looped his reins over a stunted oak. When he was sure he and Valeria were alone, he pulled her off the Ovaro's back and set her down gently. Before he could turn away, she grabbed his arm and stared up at him sheepishly.

"I just wanted to make sure you understood, Mr. Fargo. About last night . . ."

Fargo looked down at her, a gleam in his eye. "You're not that type of girl?"

She frowned, and a fire blazed in her green eyes. She hadn't bothered to put her red hair up; it cascaded richly across her shoulders. "Indeed, I'm *not*. It was the Indians and the storm . . . the strange surroundings. You could have just"—she dropped her eyes and crossed her arms on her breasts—"*reassured* me that I was safe. You needn't have . . ."

Fargo slipped his Henry repeater from the saddle sheath. "You got it, Miss Howard. Next time, instead of letting you maul me like a she-griz with the springtime craze, I'll *reassure* you that you're not about to lose your pretty hair. Now, if you'll excuse me, I'm gonna cross the stream and look around from that rise yonder, see if there's any Indians between us and the fort."

He turned to push through the cattails lining the creek, jacking a fresh round in the Henry's chamber.

"Fargo?"

He turned around. She stood beside the grazing

pinto, the sun fairly glowing in those angry, agate eyes. Her bosom rose and fell like that of an angry schoolmarm.

"I know how men like to brag about their conquests. With that in mind, I would hope that you might restrain your man's shameful impulses, and save me the indignity of spreading what happened last night around Fort Clark. I mean, even if I could bear the embarrassment, Father would—"

"This might come as a shock to you, Miss Howard," Fargo said, "but you weren't my first *conquest*, and, unless the Blackfeet and Assiniboine have something more to say on the subject, you won't be my last. Rest assured, your secret's safe with me. Now, why don't you tend nature or have a drink of water or something, and let me scout around a bit?"

He left her standing on the bank as he followed a deer path through the willows and cattails and pushed out toward the edge of the narrow, churning stream. He took the Henry in one hand, set his feet, and spread his arms.

Just as he was about to spring to the creek's other side, a scream rose from his left flank, Valeria Howard's piercing cry of sheer terror echoing around the shallow canyon.

Fargo wheeled and sprinted back the way he'd come, stumbling in the weedy turf. He ran around the pinto, which was prancing nervously and craning its neck to stare over its left hip, and plunged into the tall wheatgrass, heading upstream. Bounding over a low rise, he stopped suddenly, stared into the depression before him.

Valeria stood facing him, her face in her hands. Another fifteen feet beyond her, a man lay in the crinkled, bloodstained grass, several arrows sprouting from his chest, belly, and legs.

Beyond the body, a freight wagon sat at the edge of the brush lining the creek, two mules lying dead before the drooping wagon tongue, their bloody carcasses half concealed by young cottonwoods and willows. The tarp had come loose from the box, revealing overturned barrels and broken crates. Several more barrels and burlap bags lay scattered behind the wagon, dislodged when the freighter had tried to make a run for the creek, Indians nipping at his heels.

Fargo moved around Valeria and stood over the stout body clad in a blood-soaked wool coat, stovepipe boots, and duck trousers. He'd thought the man's head had been concealed by the brush, but he saw now that the head was gone—chopped off with a hatchet—leaving a grisly, ragged hole atop the man's broad shoulders.

Wrinkling his nose at the cloying, copper stench of fresh blood, Fargo looked around. A large cottonwood stood left of the wagon. Something had been attached to the trunk with a feathered arrow. Fargo moved down the knoll and circled the wagon, squinting at the tree trunk until the object attached to it became the head of the Frenchman's freighting partner, Jan Hallbing.

The arrow had been drilled through the man's forehead. The eyelids, brushed by wisps of wheat blond hair, drooped as though with extreme fatigue. The tongue protruded from the mouth, angled slightly as though to lick blood from the swollen lower lip. Blood dribbled from the ragged flaps of torn skin at the neck, streaking the cottonwood's trunk below.

So much for Hallbing's truce with the Assiniboine.

Fargo wheeled suddenly and peered back in the direction of the roadhouse. His heart thudded as a slender column of gray-black smoke rose in the far distance, nearly too thin to see from this vantage

41

point—a good three miles—unless you were looking for it.

The roadhouse was on fire, which probably meant that Smiley's relations with the local aborigines had chilled along with Hallbing's. Dropping his gaze and shading his eyes from the sun's glare, Fargo could make out the jostling brown blurs of distant riders moving toward him across the rolling prairie.

Galloping toward him.

"Mount up!" the Trailsman shouted as he ran back toward the pinto.

Kneeling where he'd left her, holding her arms across her stomach, Valeria turned toward him, her gaze both questioning and fearful.

"More company!"

Fargo paused to lift the girl brusquely to her feet then half dragged, half carried her over the rise to where the Ovaro waited, craning its neck to stare back toward the roadhouse. The horse had obviously scented the Indians; it twitched its ears and nickered anxiously, prancing in place.

Fargo threw the girl up behind the saddle, then grabbed the reins and swung into the leather. He didn't have to spur the horse into motion; almost before he'd gotten seated, the pinto bulled forward into the cattails and willows, leaped over the rushing creek, and bounded up the opposite side of the cut.

As the horse gained the crest of the ridge, snorting and blowing, hooves thumping, Fargo turned back to see the jostling brown blurs moving toward him. The Indians were a mile away but moving fast and spread out in a loose group, with several holding war lances or rifles.

Behind them, the smoke from Smiley's roadhouse ribboned skyward.

"What's got into those crazy savages?" Fargo muttered. He gave the pinto its head and tipped his hat brim low. The horse galloped up and down the gentle prairie knolls and hogbacks, swerving wide of the occasional alder or cottonwood copse.

With the pinto's blazing speed, it wasn't long before Fort Clark rose up out of the prairie ahead, at the confluence of two streams—Little Porcupine Creek and the Mouse River. A low jog of steep buttes rose a quarter mile from the fort's right wall, and a hat-shaped bluff towered over a cottonwood forest on the left.

Clark was a stockade-surrounded fortress hewn, adzed, and back-and-bellied from trees felled in the breaks of the Missouri River. From this distance, and even with its blockhouses and guard towers looming over its four corners, the fort appeared little more significant than a small schooner on a large sea of gray-green grass and scattered oak, cottonwood, and ash. But Fargo had never been as happy to see one of these far-flung military outposts in his life.

The happiness was short-lived.

Valeria tapped his shoulder and said in a frightened voice shaken by the horse's pounding strides, "Fargo . . . over there!"

He looked west. A half dozen painted warriors bounded over a low, rocky rise, maniacally heeling their mustangs into turf-chewing gallops, angling southeast on an interception course.

Swirling war paint glistened on their cherry red faces. Their hair—braided, feathered, greased, and trimmed with rawhide strips and bone amulets—blew out behind them. The knife slashes of their mouths spread with glory whoops and battle cries. Several braves raised their ash bows or plucked arrows from quivers flopping down their backs.

"Keep your head down!" Fargo ordered, clawing his .44 from its holster.

The pinto jerked a glance toward the Indians thundering toward them on the right, bounding over the prairie swells, their horses stretched out in long, leaping strides. The pinto gave an anxious snort and lowered its head, stretching its own legs, driving ahead even faster.

Before Fargo, the fort rose up out of the bunchgrass and wild timothy. To his right, the Indians drew within fifty yards. Several loosed arrows. They whirred like bats around the Trailsman's head, one cutting close enough that he could hear the shriek of the feathered shaft before it broke on a lone boulder to his left.

Another knifed the air just behind Valeria, who gave a miserable cry.

Fargo loosed a couple of errant shots at the Indians. They didn't so much as hesitate but continued on their driving, slanting course, which in another hundred yards would put them between the fort's front stockade wall, and Fargo.

But then the pinto began to pull away, and the Indians' cunning, kill-crazy expressions tensed. All but that of one young warrior on a small blue roan. He kept pace with the pinto.

Drawing to within thirty yards of Fargo's right stirrup, and taking his braided halter ribbons in his teeth, the glory-drunk brave knocked and cocked an arrow. Fargo extended the .44 in his right hand, aimed as well as he could from his jouncing seat, and fired.

The Colt roared. The brave loosed the arrow, which flew wildly above and behind Fargo and Valeria.

At the same time, the bullet plunked through the Indian's breastbone and drove him off the right side of his horse. As he got tangled with the roan's scissoring legs, the horse gave a shrill scream, and then horse and rider both hit the ground and rolled and somersaulted wildly, dust puffing up around their windmilling limbs and the scattering arrows as though from a cannon ball explosion.

"Ah, shit!" Fargo muttered, watching another brave whip his lathered horse up on his right and raise a Henry rifle to his shoulder.

Fargo stiffened as he saw the brave angle the barrel to deliver a killing shot to the Ovaro's beautiful head.

6

Fargo knew he had no time to shoot the brave bearing down on the Ovaro or to turn the mount away without spilling the horse, himself, and Valeria. He flicked back the Colt's hammer, angled the pistol straight out toward the brave galloping about twenty yards off Fargo's right stirrup.

Before Fargo could trigger the .44, the brave's rifle spoke.

Fargo squeezed the Colt's trigger. At the same time that the revolver leaped in his hand, the Ovaro lurched. Fargo knew his own shot had sailed wide of the brave, but the brave's rifle dropped from his hand, hit the ground, and tumbled back behind the racing mustang. Then the brave himself flew straight back off his striped blanket saddle, as though a noose had been pulled taut around his neck from behind. He rolled off the horse's rump, flew out over the tail, and hit the ground, rolling and tumbling out of sight in a sifting cloud of dust, grass, and dirt clods.

The Trailsman glanced at the pinto, relieved that the horse was still striding unharmed, snorting and blowing as it raced toward the stockade looming ahead. As Fargo's eyes raked the wall, he became aware of pistols and rifles popping and booming, smoke puffing from above the wall's pointed log tips. Several soldiers stood on the shooting ledge on the inside of the wall, and were firing over the wall toward the Indians, most of whom now drew back on their horses' reins while another screamed and flew off the back of his racing mustang.

Movement ahead caught Fargo's eye, and he turned forward to see the stockade's double doors split apart and swing toward him. Two soldiers in dark blue tunics and tan kepis pushed out between the parting doors. Two dashed right of the gate, one left, and, dropping to their knees and raising their Springfields to their shoulders, bore down on the Indians now drawing their horses to skidding halts on Fargo's right.

Atop the stockade wall, a burly, bearded gent in a leather hat and tanned buckskin jacket beckoned and shouted, "Come on, Skyeeee!" A mad guffaw vaulted above the pinto's thundering hooves, and white teeth shone in the burly gent's cinnamon beard. "You done whipped those red savages at their own game!"

More deep laughter exploded as the Ovaro raced between the soldiers, who were triggering their rifles off Fargo's right flank. The horse cleaved the open stockade doors and plunged into the fort's dusty, manure-pocked yard, turning right and grinding its hooves into the chalky turf as the Trailsman drew back on the reins.

A man shouted, *"Valeria!"*

Fargo and the girl raised their gazes to the stockade wall, where ten or twelve soldiers and a rotund hombre in smoke-tanned buckskins milled on the shooting ledge, a couple still triggering their army-issue Springfields over the wall toward the prairie.

A tall, hatless gent with thick dashing hair nearly the same red as Valeria's stood facing Fargo and the girl, holding a smoking .44 in his hand. He wore duck pants with red-stitched pockets, snakeskin spats, and a white silk shirt under a cowskin vest bearing a distinctive pinto pattern. Nothing on the man's attire indicated that he was an army major, but his red hair and fatherly gaze directed at Valeria left little doubt that the man was Major Howard, commander of Fort Clark.

"Father!" the girl sobbed, and Fargo saw her shadow on the hoof-pocked ground clap a hand to her mouth, stemming a cry of both shock and relief.

"Oh, my girl!" The major holstered his pistol and moved along the shooting ledge toward a ladder constructed of narrow logs and rawhide. "I never thought I'd see you alive!"

He descended the ladder quickly and dropped the last three feet to the ground. Fargo had dismounted the horse and was helping the girl down. She ran to her father, sobbing as the major snaked his arms around her slender waist and buried his face in her hair.

"Oh, Valeria . . . you have no idea how relieved . . ."

"Father, you wouldn't believe what happened," she cried, convulsing in the man's arms.

"Shush now," the major said, smoothing her hair against the back of her head. "You're safe now. You're here." The man glanced expectantly at Fargo as the girl's back continued jerking and muffled sobs rose from her mouth buried against the major's shoulder.

"A war party attacked us on the other side of Smiley's roadhouse," Fargo said. The shooting had died off, the Indians apparently giving up the fight, and the soldiers were closing the stockade's gate with a raspy creak of leather hinges. "Except for your daughter and me, the entire party was wiped out. We had to abandon the stage, rode like hell to the roadhouse. Spent the night there. I saw smoke from that direction earlier this morning."

Major Howard sighed darkly, his cheek still pressed to his daughter's head. "I sent couriers to warn you, but apparently they didn't make it through." He turned around. "We'll talk later this evening. I'm going to see my daughter to my cabin. See to your horse and a bath, Mr. Fargo. Then see Captain Thomas for debriefing. In the meantime, do you know Mr. Charley?"

Fargo turned in the direction indicated. The only other man Fargo had seen so far not dressed in army blues was descending the creaky ladder, huffing and puffing with the effort. At the bottom, the man in stained buckskins turned and shuffled toward him, grinning in his shaggy, cinnamon beard.

Fargo ran his gaze across the stout frame of the old army scout and tracker, and sighed ruefully. "Prairie Dog Charley. I reckon I've confessed to worse. Didn't figure the old dog was still howling on this side of the sod."

The major, leading his daughter away, said, "Mr. Charley will fill you in and show you the stables."

As Howard and Valeria drifted off toward the log huts and cabins on the north side of the parade ground, Valeria glanced back toward Fargo, a vague conspiratorial smile in her red-rimmed eyes. She turned away and rested her head once more against her father's shoulder, wrapping an arm around his waist.

Prairie Dog Charley pulled up before Fargo, grinning wolfishly after the girl, showing a full set of large, white teeth framed in glistening, brown tobacco juice. "Skye, you *didn't*?" The tracker dropped his voice and canted his head toward Fargo, so the soldiers wouldn't hear. "The major's *daughter*, fer cryin' out loud? Son, you haven't changed a bit!"

"And you have, you old whoremonger?"

Fargo ran his gaze down the burly, buckskin-clad, broad-shouldered frame, from the greasy leather hat that covered the scant hair left by a scalp-crazy Comanche down in the Texas panhandle, to his boot moccasins sewn and patched from tanned moose hide and trimmed with the ebony hair of a black panther.

A small bone-handled knife protruded from a sheath attached to the inside of the right moccasin, and around his considerable waist he wore two Colt Pattersons and a stag-handled bowie. A muzzle-loading German percussion rifle, a Schuetzen with a deeply curved and silver-fitted butt-plate, rested atop his shoulder.

"Except for wielding that prissy target piece," Fargo said, "you're still the ugly old mossy-horn I left at Fort Bliss two springs ago. No doubt still howling at full moons, too."

Prairie Dog guffawed and jostled the rifle's barrel proudly. "This here's a gift from Sir Frederick Somesuch of Manchester. Took him shooting in Colorado, don't ya know, and even though his wife tore off with a handsome Ute warrior, and the Sir hisself almost went down a wild sow griz's belly in *tiny little pieces*, he gave me this here rifle for his appreciation of my services."

The old tracker glanced at the sweat-lathered pinto standing behind Fargo, who watched both men with strained patience; the Ovaro was accustomed to a good rubdown and water after a long, hard ride. "Took down that brave aiming for your prized stallion with this here German-smithed piece, I did," Prairie Dog continued. "So mind your manners toward my gun . . . and can't you see your horse is chompin' fer a rubdown?"

"Lead the way to the stables," Fargo said, grabbing the pinto's reins. "And then the sutler's saloon. The drinks are on me, you old sharpshooting moon howler."

As Prairie Dog headed toward the stables at the north side of the compound, a couple of gaunt privates in torn uniforms and battered forage hats stepped in front of Fargo. Fargo frowned as the two hemmed and hawed nervously, shifting their weight from one foot to the other, glancing at each other as if for encouragement.

Prairie Dog howled and clapped one of the lads on the shoulder. "Oh, don't get your tongues all in a twist, boys. This here's the famous—or, I should say, the *notorious*—Trailsman, sure enough. Go ahead and take a good look at him, then git out of the way, will ya? We got work to do!"

The boys flushed and, nearly at the same time, scrubbed their hands on their threadbare tunics, then extended the dirt-encrusted paws at the Trailsman. "A pleasure to meet you, Mr. Fargo," said the taller of the two. "A real pleasure."

"We knew if anyone could bring the major's daughter through, that person would be you, sir," said the other, a scrawny lad with hair like wild oat stalks poking out from around his torn, faded hat. "Me an' Benny, we really been anticipatin' your visit."

"M-maybe you'd join us for some poker later, Mr. Fargo?" asked the taller lad. "We ain't allowed in the saloon, but we'd be right honored if you stop by the bear den later. Uh, that's the enlisted men's barracks. Maybe share some of your stories. Why, we been hearing about you since—"

"Come on now, lads!" Prairie Dog cut in, doffing his hat to swipe it against the scrawny private's shoulder. "Can't you see you're embarrassin' the man? Off with you, now. Me and Fargo got business to palaver."

"Y-yessir!" said the blond private, both young soldiers shuffling off toward the parade ground where drills were resuming after the Indian scare. "Sorry, sir."

"Didn't mean to pester you, Mr. Fargo!"

"I might just join you for that poker game," Fargo called after them. "If old Prairie Dog is true to form, he'll no doubt bore my socks off long before sundown!"

Fargo snorted and clapped a hand to Prairie Dog's shoulder as they continued toward the stables. Blue smoke ribboned from several of the stone chimneys surrounding the parade ground and from a cook pit before the mess hall. A man in bloodstained buckskins carved a deer outside the sutler's store while a half-breed woman in bright calico rolled the freshly cut roasts in burlap.

Leading the pinto through the wide gap between the sutler's store and the officers' cabins, Fargo asked Prairie Dog what had set the Indians to stomping with their tails up, and which tribes were involved.

Prairie Dog swiped a hand across his beard and shook his head. "The major'll fill you in this evening, Skye. It ain't purty. I'll tell ya that."

"That's why I want it from you. In plain talk, no army bullshit."

As they entered the cool shadows of the remount barn, the clang of a smithy's hammer rising from the nearby blacksmith shop, Prairie Dog hiked a hip on the edge of a water barrel. "We been havin' trouble off and on for three weeks. That's when the Assiniboine started raiding the trading posts and little settlements popping up along the creeks and streams.

"We didn't think we had a *serious* problem till an

eight-man woodcutting crew was sent out last week and never came back. We found 'em butchered in a ravine about three miles west, along Squaw Creek. Decapitated. Mutilated in ways I ain't even seen the Comanches do. Their mules shot, wagons burned. Then, three days ago, we spied smoke rising from the direction of our sister fort, William, down along Little Muddy Creek."

About to set his saddle on a stall partition, Fargo froze and glanced sharply at the old scout. "They *burned* Fort William?"

Prairie Dog shook his head. "Don't know for sure. I rode out to have a look, and the Injuns—more'n a dozen mixed Assiniboine and Blackfeet—chased me back, killin' my pony in the run. Lost the three boys who rode with me."

The old scout squinted one eye and gestured with his hand. "I *can* tell you *this* about William—we ain't seen hide nor hair of their soldiers since we spied the smoke, and we usually exchanged couriers daily. Since another patrol was wiped out day before yesterday, Major Howard's ordered the gates closed. No one leaves till we can come up with a way to turn those savages' horn back in. We have little hope of help from outside, as we can't get couriers through to the forts along the Missouri."

Fargo set the saddle across the stall partition, then grabbed a burlap sack from the hay-flecked floor. Brows ridged with consternation, he set to work rubbing down the pinto's sleek, sweat-lathered coat. "You still haven't told me what got those Injuns' tails in a twist, hoss."

"That's the ugliest part of this bailiwick, Skye." Prairie Dog picked up a handful of dry straw and went to work on the Ovaro's hindquarters, scrubbing off the lathered, muddy sweat. "One of our own men might've riled those savages. A lieutenant named Mordecai Duke."

The Trailsman frowned and glanced around the Ovaro's head at Prairie Dog. "Duke? Seems I heard that name before."

"He was once a fine officer. Straight outta West Point. His family ran a shipping business in New York. Friends of all the mucky-mucks. Hell of an Indian fighter, old Mordecai. Till he went crazier'n a tree full of owls."

The old scout stopped working to lift his hat from his horribly scarred scalp and run a gloved hand through the remaining salt-and-pepper hair tufting up around the knotted, grisly scars. "He went so nuts, drinkin' like a fish, laughin' and cryin' by fits, that the major decided to ship him back to St. Louis, to some special institution for army officers who got their bellies a little too full of the frontier life . . . if you're gettin' my drift."

With his index finger, Prairie Dog made a swirling motion in front of his ear. "He wasn't more than twenty miles southwest of the fort when he broke out of the wagon, killed two of the guards with his bare hands, and hightailed it into the tall-and-uncut, like a mustang with tin cans tied to its tail."

"Well, how in the hell . . . ?" Fargo let his voice trail off, pricking his ears. Voices rose from beyond the barn's open doors, growing louder as men approached.

Prairie Dog glanced outside, then turned to the Trailsman and said softly, "Best not talk about this in front of the enlisted boys. They don't know about Lieutenant Duke and the Injuns. Let's finish up here, and we'll finish our powwow over a drink in the sutler's saloon."

While Prairie Dog smoked a cigarette outside the

barn, the Trailsman finished rubbing down the Ovaro, stabling it, and measuring out oats, hay, and water. He told the remount sergeant, an irreverent, craggy-faced Scot named Drake, to turn the pinto into the corral after the mount had cooled off and had eaten and drunk its measured portions.

"Don't put him out with any mares in rut," Fargo warned as he grabbed his rifle and saddlebags. "Once he sets his hat for a filly, it'll take a dozen men to change his mind."

He moved off down the barn alley, the crotchety Scot grumbling his displeasure at taking orders from a civilian while running a file across the horse hoof wedged between his knees.

7

Fargo and Prairie Dog tramped over to the sutler's store in the early afternoon sunshine. The two-story log structure with a lean-to addition housing the saloon was shaded by a giant cottonwood tree rustling its silver leaves in the perpetual prairie breeze.

The store smelled like molasses and flour and cured meat. The Trailsman and Prairie Dog were the only saloon customers at this hour. They sat at a table under a large bison trophy mounted on a square-hewn ceiling joist. Through the open shutters emanated the phlegmatic barks of an infantry sergeant, the thuds of an ax, and the occasional stamp of horses passing the store on cavalry drill.

Between the sounds was an eerie, tense silence, as if the fort were awaiting an Indian attack similar to the one on Fort William. In the blockhouses, the guards had been doubled or tripled, and extra soldiers were perched on the shooting ledges along the stockade walls, facing the endless swell of prairie around the fort.

The sutler's stoic Indian wife brought Fargo and Prairie Dog each a schooner of surprisingly cold ale and a whiskey shot. Collecting Fargo's coins, she shuffled sullenly back to the store, where she'd been tying and wrapping the deer roasts her husband had carved from the carcass outside.

Fargo sipped the whiskey suspiciously, made a face as he swallowed. "Did Smiley Bristo have a whiskey contract with the sutler, by any chance?"

Prairie Dog downed nearly half of his own shot, and smacked his lips. "Nectar of the gods, ain't it?"

"Wrathful gods," Fargo muttered, and washed down the camphorlike taste of the liquor with several deep swallows of the wheaty, refreshing beer. Setting the mug down, he tossed his hat on a chair and sank back in his seat. "Finish the story, hoss—what's this crazy Lieutenant Duke have to do with the uprising?"

Prairie Dog tossed down his own hat and fingered the tooth dangling from his right ear. He claimed it was a tooth from the Comanche who had scalped him down in Texas. When he'd looked around the saloon, making sure that he and Fargo were alone, he propped his elbows on the table, looked across at the Trailsman with a serious expression, and kept his voice low.

"You see, Lieutenant Duke spent a lot of time with a band of Assiniboine camped on the far side of Squaw Creek. Now, that's against regulations, and most of this is hearsay, but rumor has it he married the daughter of Chief Iron Shirt. Iron Shirt took a liking to the lieutenant, even though Duke was obviously crazier than a pack of wild lobos on the night of the first full moon. Or maybe *because* he was crazy. The Injuns often take craziness for wisdom, don't you know?"

Fargo nodded. He'd been around Indians enough to know that men and women whom white folks would normally lock up in a funny farm were often given special privileges amongst the natives. Many were respected for their "crazy wisdom" and insight into the "ether regions." Some tribal leaders had been known to call upon these people for advice on hunting or battle strategies or to cast spells on their enemies.

"To make a long story short," Prairie Dog continued, "Lieutenant Duke and Iron Shirt have been seen riding together with a whole passel of painted warriors. Apparently, somehow, Lieutenant Duke—in his crazy, mixed-up mind—decided the Indians oughta be killin' the whites. And, somehow, he got the Blackfeet to throw in with the Assiniboine to do just that."

"Two tribes that normally fight each other," Fargo said, daring another sip of the rotgut whiskey. "You reckon the major's attempt to trot Duke off to a nuthouse turned him against the entire army?"

"And the poor white settlers and trappers in these parts," Prairie Dog said. "Possible." He chased the whiskey with the beer, draining his schooner in three long chugs, then plunked the glass back down on the table. "Now, ain't this a fine sichy-ation?"

"You have any idea what the major intends to do about it?"

Prairie Dog grinned. "No. But I got a feelin' it's gonna involve you, Mr. Trailsman, sir." He slid his chair back. "Now, if you'll excuse this rancid old hide, I'm due over to Lieutenant Donovan's office to see about puttin' a huntin' expedition together. One that won't lose its hair and other sundry body parts. We have enough food for a few more days, but sooner or later we're gonna need meat."

Fargo lifted his beer glass. "I reckon I'll have a bath and a shave. Bathhouse still by sud's row?"

"It is. And don't forget to see Captain Thomas for your 'debriefing.'"

"Hell," Fargo grunted, donning his hat and rising. "I'm between contracts. If the captain wants to debrief me, he can come looking for me. I'm gonna take a good long bath and a nap before heading over to the major's this evening." He paused beside Prairie Dog in the store's open doorway, looking out at the sun-washed parade ground. "You'll be there?"

"Ain't been invited yet, but I probably will be. Howard's probably gonna try to throw me in with you, for no more pay than what I'm gettin' now!" Prairie Dog cursed, descended the porch steps, and sauntered off across the parade ground where a dozen soldiers marched, the sun reflecting off their rifles and sabers.

Fargo enjoyed a long, hot bath in the bathhouse at the south end of the fort. Through the room's single window, he watched the three stout wash ladies—the wives of noncoms—stirring kettles of boiling uniforms over ash wood fires while telling bawdy stories they didn't think anyone could overhear, and laughing with salty abandon.

After the bath, he sacked out in a bunk at the back of the sutler's store—just a storeroom cluttered with barrels, crates, and flour sacks—but far enough from the fort's fray that he slept soundly until the light angling through the window was the salmon hue of late afternoon. Desultory voices rose from the saloon on the other side of the wall—the voices of officers finally freed from their duty and seeking distraction from the Indian trouble in the saloon's questionable liquor.

Fargo stepped into fresh buckskins, donned his hat, and, leaving his rifle and saddlebags in the care of the sutler, headed off to Major Howard's cabin on the north side of the parade ground. The two-story structure sat about halfway down the row of officers' cabins, and could be distinguished from the others by its larger size and grand fieldstone hearth abutting the east end. It also had a broader porch and a brick-lined path leading from the front porch, around a well-

tended thicket of prairie rosebushes and chrysanthe-
mums, to a two-seater privy out back.

Valeria Howard answered Fargo's knock on the
door and regarded him coolly, holding the door only
two feet wide, as though she weren't sure she would
let him in. She glanced quickly behind her, then tipped
her head forward, and whispered, "You haven't told
anyone, have you?"

Fargo grinned and dropped his eyes to her bosom
heaving behind a delightfully low-cut dinner dress.
The ample breasts were pushed up and out, to thrilling
effect. The ribbon choker on her neck, adorned with
an ivory cameo resting just beneath the small mole on
her neck, complemented the outfit nicely. Her rich,
red hair was piled in a loose bun atop her head. Re-
acting to his bald appraisal, a blush rose in her finely
tapered cheeks.

He wanted to grab her, tear her hair free of its bun,
lift her skirts, and kiss that wide, delectable mouth.

Instead, he grunted and shifted his weight from one
boot to the other. "Don't flatter yourself." He returned
his eyes to hers. "You were one hell of a romp—and
I'd put you high on my list of the best I've had—but it
wasn't anything I'd squawk about. Now, can I come in,
or do you wanna send a plate out to the porch?"

Green eyes flashing angrily, she stepped back and
jerked the door wide. "Do come in, Mr. Fargo!"

The Trailsman gave his boots an obligatory scrape
on the porch boards, doffed his hat, and stepped over
the threshold. He found himself in the cabin's simple,
rustic but comfortable kitchen, which was warm from
the ticking iron range against the far wall, and rife
with the smell of roasting meat.

A stout, gray-haired woman in a bonnet and apron
stood at a table slicing a steaming bread loaf—another

noncom's wife, probably, working as the major's housekeeper. Fargo had heard that the major's own wife, Valeria's mother, had years ago died from a fever back east. Valeria had been educated at the best boarding and finishing schools. She'd come to Fort Howard to spend the summer with her father before traveling with wealthy friends overseas.

"The men are in the *parlor*," Valeria curtly announced, staring up at Fargo icily. "Dinner will be served shortly."

"Obliged," Fargo said, nodding at the housekeeper who'd looked up from her work to greet the newcomer with a wan smile.

Hooking his hat on a rack, Fargo turned through a door in the kitchen's left wall, and entered the nattily-appointed parlor where four men—Major Howard, Prairie Dog Charley, and two crisply dressed officers—stood in a tight clump before a red divan and a ticking wall clock. There was a thick throw rug on the floor beneath their boots. Beyond them, through an open door, lay the dining room in which a long table stood draped with oilcloth and china place settings.

"Ah, Mr. Fargo," the Major said, halting his hushed conversation midsentence. "How good of you to join us."

The others turned toward the Trailsman, including Prairie Dog Charley, all holding glasses quarter filled with whiskey or brandy, and smoldering cigars. Prairie Dog gave Fargo a furtive wink.

"Do come in and meet Captain Rudolph Thomas and Lieutenant Andrew Ryan. Gentlemen, meet Skye Fargo, commonly referred to as the Trailsman."

Fargo shook hands first with Ryan—a slender, prematurely balding man in his late twenties—and then Thomas, who quirked his upswept mustache in a stiff smile as he said, "Ah, yes, the Trailsman. We were to meet earlier for your debriefing, Mr. Fargo, but I couldn't find you anywhere."

Thomas was also in his late twenties—short and pale and bespectacled, with a flawless uniform and a smattering of red pimples across his cheekbones. He and Ryan were obviously West Point lads. They'd come west to bludgeon the savage redskins, but now, realizing they'd had no idea what they'd gotten themselves into nor of the Indians' fighting abilities and furor, were soiling their trousers hourly. Their faces were stiff, smiles taut, eyes glassy.

"Sorry, Captain," Fargo grunted, releasing the man's hand. "There wasn't much to debrief. We were ambushed, everyone in our party dead but myself and Miss Howard. I had a bath and took a nap in the sutler's storeroom."

Prairie Dog chuckled as he lifted his glass to his bearded mouth.

Turning away to fill a goblet from a cut-glass decanter, Major Howard said, "The sutler's storeroom? Mr. Fargo, we've humble accommodations, to be sure, but we can certainly put you up better than that!"

Fargo hiked a shoulder as he accepted the glass. "I like bein' out of the way." He sipped the whiskey, which was better than that in the sutler's saloon. "Prairie Dog here filled me in on the Indian trouble, Major. I know from being out there myself that you're pretty well surrounded. Any ideas about how you're gonna get yourself out of this bailiwick?"

The major flushed slightly as he glanced at the other two officers. They and Prairie Dog stood before Fargo in a loose semicircle. Returning his gaze to the tall Trailsman standing before them in smoke-stained buckskins and with a no-nonsense scowl on his rugged features, the major chuckled. "You like getting to the point, don't you? Well, shall we have a seat, gentlemen? I'd been going to save this part of the conversation until *after* we'd dined, but since Mr. Fargo would like to skin the cat now, let's skin it now."

Fargo sat in a bullhorn rocking chair near the front window. When the lieutenant, the captain, and Prairie Dog had taken seats around him, the major refilled their glasses and sat in a cowhide chair to Fargo's right. He jerked his gold-buttoned tunic down sharply, cleared his throat, and propped a low-heeled cavalry boot on a knee.

Since Prairie Dog had already briefed Fargo on the situation, Howard merely summarized the trouble from the start of the uprising to present, adding nothing Fargo didn't already know, including his suspicions about the insane Lieutenant Duke.

"Which leads me to the reason I'd like to extend your contract, Mr. Fargo," the major said, puffing his stogie, a sheepish cast entering his eyes as he shifted his gaze to the two other officers.

The major paused as if for dramatic effect, and Fargo frowned impatiently. He could occasionally tolerate coyness in a woman, but not in a man. "And that is . . . ?"

Howard returned his gaze to Fargo, flinched slightly at the coldness in the Trailsman's stare, and nervously flicked ashes into the stone tray on his chair arm. "We'd like you to hunt him down and kill him."

Fargo was genuinely shocked. "*Kill* him?" He'd thought the man was going to ask him to try and run the Indians' gauntlet and seek help from an outlying fort, possibly Fort Buford or from one of the fledgling Canadian outposts on the other side of the border. "It seems to me, from what I've heard so far of this

Lieutenant Duke's relationship with Iron Shirt and the rest of his band, the last thing you'd want to do is *martyr* the man."

"We've discussed the matter thoroughly, Mr. Fargo," interjected Captain Thomas, adjusting his spectacles. "Believe me, we do not take the matter lightly."

"We considered the possibility of sending you through the Indians' lines for help," added Lieutenant Ryan. "The problem is . . . and as you doubtless know . . . the Indians *have* no lines. We've sent four men to tackle the same job . . ."

"And all four were sent back," Prairie Dog piped up when the lieutenant's voice began to quiver and fade, his cheeks blanching. "At least, their *heads* and *hearts* were sent back, dangling from their saddle horns."

Now, that was a bit of information the old cuss had been holding on to.

"I don't guarantee I'd make it, but I made it here, and I know the country," Fargo said. "If I traveled at night . . ."

"Even if you made it through," Howard said, "the help you sought wouldn't make it here in time. The Indians have been moving closer to the fort every day. At night, their council fires are quite visible in the hills beyond Squaw Creek. I'm guessing that in two, maybe three—"

The major paused when Valeria poked her head in the door. "Gentlemen, dinner will be served."

When the girl withdrew into the kitchen, Howard shuttled his glance to Fargo and the others, brows ridged with annoyance and enervation. "Shall we save the rest of the conversation for after dinner, gentlemen . . . ?"

Fargo set his glass on the decanter's silver tray and followed the others into the dining room. The meal was medallions of venison with wild onions, potatoes and gravy, fresh bread, and spinach from the fort's garden.

The food was good and rib-sticking, but Fargo was bored with the falsely-jovial dinner conversation and forced small talk. The men, including Prairie Dog, obviously had their minds on the Indians. All except Lieutenant Ryan, that was. The young soldier, obviously smitten by Valeria, offered several embarrassing questions about her schooling and travels and the possibility of their having mutual acquaintances back east, while his nearsighted gaze raked her opulent bosom. Valeria answered the questions politely, picking at her food and flicking her own oblique gazes across the table at the Trailsman, doing little to encourage the randy young officer's pursuit.

After dessert of canned peach pie and coffee, the girl excused herself to help the cook, Mildred, clear the table and wash the dishes and clean the kitchen. Major Howard poured Fargo and the other men a fresh glass before retaking his chair with a sigh, and regarding the Trailsman with gravity from across the table. Pensively, he tapped the rim of his glass.

The others sat in their chairs like statues.

Howard said, "Mr. Fargo, it's with a deep reluctance and a heavy heart that I'm ordering the assassination of one of my own men. Before he went crazy, Lieutenant Duke and I were very close. We played chess nearly every evening. He was a master of the game. He tended to idealize the Indians, seemed to fancy becoming one himself, but otherwise a sensible, likable young man.

"However, he has gone quite insane. And for some reason, he has become a shaman of sorts to Chief Iron Shirt, ostensibly encouraging the extermination of all whites from the region. I believe—and if I'm wrong I take full responsibility—that without him, Iron Shirt will pull his horns in, and he and his Blackfoot allies will disappear back into the hills beyond Squaw Creek, where they live when they're not following the buffalo."

Fargo glanced at Prairie Dog, who stared glumly down at his whiskey.

"I see your reasoning, Major." Fargo flipped his spoon in the air. "And, while I'm no regulator—never been able to stomach the breed, in fact—I'll take the job. But from what you've told me, I think there's a real danger of turning the lieutenant into a martyr. We could rile those Injuns even more, paint this prairie red with white men's blood for years to come."

Lieutenant Ryan stared at Fargo, his spectacles reflecting the dancing candlelight. He looked as though he'd been slapped, but he nodded weakly. "It's a risk we have to take. The major and I and Captain Thomas see no other options."

Captain Thomas fingered a pimple on his left cheek, stifled a yawn. "Agreed."

Major Howard sucked a fresh stogie. "As it happens, you may not have to assassinate him yourself." He glanced at Prairie Dog, who turned the corners of his mouth down. "You may have seen Mr. Charley's fancy, German-made rifle. Good from five hundred yards, the scout tells me."

"Why did I have to go braggin' about that piece?" Prairie Dog chuffed and turned to Fargo. "Well, there you have it. You're the scout, Skye. I'm the assassin. If'n you can get me within range of Iron Shirt's encampment. I've been all over this country east of the creek, but rarely west. Besides, while my eyes are eagle-sharp, the hearing in my left ear is goin'. Even if I knew the country, my poor hearing could cost me my hair not a mile from the fort."

Fargo threw back his whiskey and set his glass on

the oilcloth. "I appreciate the meal and the whiskey, Major, but I'm ready for bed." He glanced at Prairie Dog. "Clean old Betsy tonight, and let's ride out a good two hours before first light tomorrow."

"Throw down here, Mr. Fargo," Major Howard offered. "I have an extra bedroom upstairs. It would be my honor."

Fargo glanced at the ceiling and fought back a blush. Valeria would be rooming up there. No point in risking a bullet from the major in the middle of the night.

The Trailsman slid his chair back, rising. "The sutler's cot's right cozy."

"Brunhilda."

He glanced at Prairie Dog scowling up at him. "Huh?"

"The Schuetzen's name is Brunhilda." The old scout grinned. "German, don't ya know? And don't you worry—she'll be cleaned, oiled, loaded, and ready to go!"

Chuckling, Fargo excused himself, and went into the kitchen. Valeria wasn't there—only the housekeeper, singing softly to herself while shelving clean plates above the range.

Fargo thanked the woman for the good cooking and headed outside into the still prairie gloaming, the drum roll of "Twilight Tattoo" rising from the parade ground. He hitched his cartridge belt high on his hips and peered west.

Beyond the far stockade wall, the sky glowed umber though the sun had set an hour ago. His keen ears picked up the heartlike thump of war drums, barely audible above the nearer strains of "Tattoo."

8

The Trailsman stepped off the major's porch and began tramping west along the parade ground's north edge. To his right, several men moved out of the officers' quarters, some flanked by their wives, to peer pensively west, toward the flickering firelight and the eerie, primitive drum cadence.

On the south side of the parade ground, noncoms and enlisted men wandered out of their barracks, muttering curiously, some smoking or holding tin coffee cups, suspenders hanging off their shoulders, hair tussled by the warm spring breeze.

Fargo approached the stockade wall where soldiers were clumped along the shooting ledge, staring west and whispering. He climbed a ladder and moved left along the ledge, toward three young soldiers huddled together, speaking in low, enervated tones. One held a quirley to his lips as he and the others peered over the wall's sharpened log tips.

"Put out that cigarette, soldier," Fargo admonished.

The three privates jerked their heads toward him with a start. The quirley dropped to the floor of the ledge, sparking, and the lanky private crushed it under the heel of a scuffed brogan.

Peering west, Fargo said, "One of you boys have a spyglass?"

The soldiers shuffled around to his left, and then a brass-chased binocular was thrust at the Trailsman's shoulder. He grabbed it, extended it toward the glow, and adjusted the focus.

"How long you been hearing the drums?"

One of the privates sniffed and whispered, "Just a few minutes, sir. It started about the same time our boys laid in with 'Tattoo.' "

"We seen the fires before," said one of the others, "but we haven't heard the drums. They must be movin' closer."

Fargo aimed the glass at the umber glow and, twisting the canister slightly, brought up three separate red smudges amongst the dark brown hills about two and a half miles west. The sky above and behind the hills was green with the fading dusk, but the fires stood out on a hill shoulder swathed in brush and gnarled trees.

Fargo couldn't see much from this distance, but the shadows flickering before the fires were no doubt the silhouettes of dancing Indians.

A war dance.

A young man's voice trembled. "Y-you think they're going to attack the fort, sir?"

"They might just be trying to make you soil your trousers, but I'd keep my eyes peeled." Fargo reduced the spyglass and gave it back to the soldier. "Stay awake and don't fire any quirleys. The Injuns'll use 'em for target practice."

Fargo moved back along the shooting ledge, descended the ladder, and tramped off between the guardhouse and the infirmary, heading for the stables. He'd check to make sure the Ovaro was well cared for and not getting into trouble, then, since he had to be up before dawn, bed down early in the sutler's storeroom.

He found the stables dark and untended, the Ovaro in the rear paddock with about five other horses, all geldings. While the other horses munched hay or drew water or milled along the corral slats, the pinto stared tensely west, flicking its ears at the war drums that Fargo could no longer hear.

"Easy, boy," Fargo said, dropping a loop over the pinto's head and giving a gentle tug. He'd stable the horse for the night to make sure it was well rested by morning. "They're a long way off . . . for now," he added as the horse clomped through the open double doors and onto the hard-packed floor of the barn alley.

Leading the horse into a corner stable a good distance from the other stabled stock, Fargo wondered what kind of nightmares the pinto would have tonight if it knew where they'd be heading before dawn.

He'd filled the stock troughs, gave the horse's neck a good-night pat, and was backing out of the stall when he heard the crackling rustle of a foot on the straw-covered floor. Fargo moved his hand from the stable door to his pistol grips, wheeling on his heels.

"Skye?" It was Valeria's silky voice. She stood a few feet from the stable, silhouetted by a sashed window behind her.

The Trailsman sighed, dropped his hand from his pistol grips. "Shouldn't sneak up on a man. Especially with Injuns about, beatin' on war drums."

She stepped forward, into a shaft of ambient light, and extended a burlap sack. "I brought some food for tomorrow—some venison, which Mrs. Hildebrand jerked herself, and buttermilk biscuits. A couple pieces of pie for you and Mr. . . . uh"—she smiled, green eyes slitting beguilingly—"Prairie Dog."

"Hell," Fargo said, taking the bag by the twisted, twine-wrapped neck. "I'm much obliged. You must be feeling a little more neighborly since this afternoon."

Crossing her hands before her, she dropped her chin demurely. "Yes, I wanted to apologize for my demeanor. I've been through a lot lately, as you know, and I'm afraid my nerves are stretched a little taut."

Fargo dropped the bag to his side. "Apology accepted."

She stared up at him.

"Was there something else, Miss Howard?"

"No." She backed away slowly, continuing to stare up at him. "No . . . I just wanted to apologize and wish you luck on your mission. I overheard you and Father and the other men in the dining room. It sounds terribly dangerous."

Fargo moved toward her, his broad shadow falling across her willowy, high-busted frame. She wore the same low-cut dress as before, a thin veil draped carelessly across her shoulders. Unlike before, she wore no corset, and her nipples pushed out from behind the cloth like bone buttons. "That all you came for?"

"What on earth do you mean?" Even shaded by the Trailsman's broad shadow, Valeria's green eyes flashed angrily. "What happened before, Mr. Fargo, was entirely due to my . . . my *disorientation.*"

"In that case, you wouldn't want to repeat it."

Her breasts rose and fell sharply. She glanced around, then returned her gaze to Fargo's. There was little conviction in her voice. "Of course not. What do you take me for?"

Fargo pulled her taut against him and ran his hands down her sides to her hips. Lifting her skirt, he reached beneath the fine material, ran his palms along the backs of her smooth thighs and warm, naked buttocks.

71

His face only inches from hers, he grinned. "Disoriented enough to forget to wear underwear when you visit a man in a horse barn?"

He engulfed her in his arms. A gasp escaped her lips as Fargo closed his mouth over hers. As he kissed her, he peeled the dress off her shoulders and caressed her breasts, the nipples rising and pebbling against his palms.

"Not here," she groaned. "Good Lord—it's a *barn*."

"Few hotels hereabouts." Fargo crouched, picked her up, then swung around, pushing through the open door of the stable beside the Ovaro's.

Kneeling, he lay Valeria down in a low mound of hay. She rose quickly, scampered onto her knees, thrusting her hands at the buckle of his cartridge belt. Fargo sagged back in the hay as the girl tossed his gun belt aside, unbuttoned his buckskins, and began pulling the breeches down his thighs while probing around inside his underwear for his shaft.

She'd no sooner found what she was looking for than her lips slipped over the head and her tongue began its beguiling work as her mouth slid slowly down toward his crotch, her red hair cascading across his thighs.

As her head moved up and down, Fargo leaned back on his elbows. She worked him until he was grinding his molars and digging his heels into the hay. She lifted her head suddenly and scowled up at him, pouting, lips glistening.

"You bastard!"

Bare breasts jostling, she straddled him, lifted her skirts, and, holding the base of his member with one hand, lowered herself slowly, groaning and sighing until she sat snugly atop his thighs, plundering her silky, wet depths with his iron-hard shaft.

"I once had dignity," she moaned, rising on her

haunches as she lowered her mouth to his, nibbling his lips. "I've let you turn me into a wanton *hussy*, and I won't even be able to *enjoy* you anymore, because you'll be dead in a few short *hours*!"

"Easy," Fargo grunted. "It doesn't bend that way!"

"Shut up and despoil me!" She rose quickly, descended slowly, digging her fingers into his shoulders while peppering his face with hot, wet kisses. "Ohh . . . you *bastard*!"

When she came, she threw her head back, breasts out, and shook as though lightning-struck. The shuddering tickled him deep in his loins and ignited his own explosion, his juices firing like bullets rattled from the maw of a repeating rifle.

She shook even more violently, mouth wide, her fingernails on the verge of opening wounds in his shoulders. Her knees were clamped viselike against his ribs.

A horsy snort rose above and behind her, and Fargo opened his eyes. The Ovaro stared down at him from the opposite stall, a slightly incriminating, ironic cast to his gaze.

Fargo shrugged. The girl sagged down atop him, pressing her breasts against his chest and burying her face in his neck. "Oh, Skye . . . do you *have* to go out there tomorrow?"

"I accepted the assignment."

"You've seen how dangerous it is."

"I reckon if Lieutenant Duke isn't defused, he'll lead those Indians right up to the gates of this fort and beyond."

She lifted her head, listening. Clear and thin on the air came the deep-throated throbbing of distant drums. Valeria shivered and placed her hands on either side of the Trailsman's broad face.

She turned his head from side to side for emphasis,

a sharp, beseeching tone in her voice. "You come back to me—do you hear? I know what I said before, but the fact is I'm smitten and I don't care if you know it"—she quirked the corners of her mouth, and her eyes glistened in the gray shafts from the windows—"or take advantage of me."

He smoothed the rich red locks away from her cheeks. "I'll give it my best shot."

She kissed him, began to rise. "I told Mrs. Hildebrand I was just stepping out for some air. I'd better get back before Father sends out a search party."

She winked and tossed her hair back from her shoulders. Crouching, bending those fine, creamy legs, she retrieved her dress from the stable floor, then turned to the horse staring at her with brazen interest. Chuckling and clutching the dress to her breasts, she placed a tender kiss on the Ovaro's nose.

The horse snorted and brushed a hoof against the stall partition.

Valeria laughed. "You and your horse are cut from the same cloth, Mr. Fargo."

Valeria turned away from both Fargo and the horse, shook out the dress, and dropped it over her head. When she lowered her chin to begin buttoning up, Fargo pulled his pants up, climbed to his feet, snaked his arms under hers, and took her tender orbs in his hands once more, nuzzling her neck.

She pressed her hands over his and relaxed against him, tipping her head to one side.

In the distance, a man yelled and a rifle report rent the quiet night.

Valeria gasped. The Trailsman lifted his head, pricking his ears.

More shots and shouts followed by an Indian war whoop.

Valeria whipped around toward Fargo, covering her

breasts with her hands. "Oh, my God—they're attacking the fort!"

"Stay here!"

As the Ovaro nickered and jerked its head up and down, Fargo grabbed his cartridge belt, wrapped it around his waist, donned his hat, and bolted out the stall door.

"Skye, don't leave me!"

Fargo turned back to her. Valeria faced him, hands cupping her breasts. Outside, rifles and pistols popped and boomed and the shouting and whooping rose to a cacophony.

Fargo grabbed his pistol from its holster, spun the cylinder. He wished he had the Henry that he'd left in the sutler's storeroom. "Stay down and don't come out till I tell you it's clear!"

He wheeled and ran to the near end of the barn, pushed through the double doors. An arrow whistled past his right ear and twanged into the door behind him.

Fargo flinched, raised his revolver toward the dark, painted brave standing fifteen feet in front of him who was reaching behind his back for another arrow. Fargo's .44 roared, and the Indian flew back against the wall of another stock barn.

Fargo turned right, shot two more braves running toward him from the north, laying them both out with single rounds through their chests, and peered toward the fort's north stockade wall—or the short stretch he could see from between the stock barns.

Three soldiers stood on the shooting ledge, yelling and firing their rifles over the wall's sharpened log ends. One had just turned away to reload his rifle when his head snapped toward his right shoulder, a bloody arrow point jutting from the side of his head.

As the soldier fell from the shooting ledge, the

Trailsman broke into a hard sprint for the wall. Ahead, another soldier screamed as an arrow thumped into his neck, driving him back off the ledge to hit the ground on his back, writhing.

The dark head of an Indian appeared above the wall, between two red hands grabbing log points, one hand also holding a war hatchet. As the brave leaped over the wall, shrieking demonically, another bolted over the wall beside him to smash a tomahawk into the head of a sergeant who'd dropped to one knee to reload his Springfield. The hatchet nearly cleaved the soldier's hatted head in two, killing him instantly.

Fargo stopped and, cursing, shot the brave who'd killed the sergeant, his round plunking through the Indian's right ear to splash another wall-leaping brave with blood and brains. Fargo turned to shoot another brave, ducked to avoid a war hatchet somersaulting toward him, then blew the brave back off the wall with two hastily fired .44 rounds.

Fargo looked left and up.

A screaming brave leaped toward him, the feathered spear in the Indian's right hand angled toward the Trailsman's chest. Fargo snapped off the Colt's last shot, drilling a small, dark hole in the brave's upper middle chest. Dropping the empty revolver, he threw up both hands, grabbing the dying brave's left arm and spear hand, thrusting the spear to one side as the painted, grease-coated body bulled him off his feet and into the ground on his back.

Fargo rolled the brave's writhing, grunting body off his chest, glancing right and left along the stockade wall. Small clumps of soldiers fought the Indians leaping the wall from the backs of their galloping mounts, arrows whistling while rifles and pistols popped and flashed in the twilight.

Amidst the yells to his right, Fargo heard the rumbling curses of Prairie Dog Charley between angry pistol barks and above the shouted Irish-accented commands of a sergeant encouraging his men against the storming hoard of shrieking natives.

Spying a brave aiming a nocked arrow at him from the shooting ledge, Fargo grabbed a war hatchet embedded in the ground near his right shoulder, and heaved it. At the same time the hatchet buried its head into the brave's chest, his arrow twanging into the ground beside Fargo's right knee, a high-pitched scream rose above the cacophony.

A woman's scream.

"Skye!" It was Valeria. *"Help meeeeee!"*

9

Rising to a knee, Fargo looked to his right, in the direction from which Valeria had screamed.

"Skye!" she cried again.

About thirty yards away, a howling brave broke out from between the hay stables, sprinting toward a ladder leaning against the stockade wall, carrying Valeria across his right shoulder.

"The major's daughter!" a soldier shouted beyond the running Indian, his voice nearly drowned by the gunfire and yowling savages.

Fargo slipped his Arkansas toothpick from his boot and sprinted after the girl. Above and left, a brave leaped over the wall and dropped onto the shooting platform. The brave loosed an arrow at Fargo. He ducked as the arrow shrieked over his head and plunked into a stable wall. Another brave leaped off the shooting wall and into Fargo's path. Fargo stopped, pulled his hips back as the Indian slashed at him with a bone-handled knife, then drove the toothpick into the brave's bare belly.

The Indian howled like a gut-shot coyote.

Shoving the brave back against the stockade wall, Fargo pulled his toothpick free of the man's entrails, and continued sprinting. The Indian carrying Valeria was halfway up the wall when Fargo reached the ladder. Pounding her fists against the Indian's bare, glistening back, Valeria's gaze met Fargo's, her green eyes alight with bone-rending terror.

"Skyyyyyyyye!"

Fargo leaped up the ladder, slashing at the Indian's calves with the toothpick but missing, catching the toothpick's sharp blade into the hide attaching the rungs to the two cottonwood poles. Around him, men were shooting and shouting. Out of nowhere, an Indian grabbed Fargo from behind and pulled him down the ladder, battering the Trailsman's head and shoulders with his bare fists.

At the base of the ladder, Fargo whipped around and drove his right boot into the Indian's jaw. As the brave stumbled straight back, groaning and clutching his face, Fargo lunged up the ladder's squawking rungs, using his arms as much as his feet.

Above, the Indian carrying Valeria dropped a leg over the stockade wall. Valeria clutched the pointed log tips as the Indian pulled her over the top. Fargo thrust his right arm at Valeria's hand, wrapped his fingers around hers.

The girl screamed as her fingers slipped from Fargo's. Fargo lunged for her hand once more. But it was gone, leaving only the sharpened log ends she'd been clutching and a couple of strands of long red hair wisping from slivers.

The shooting ledge bounced and shuddered beneath the Trailsman's boots. He looked around. Braves ran toward him from both sides of the ledge.

Fargo grabbed a Colt revolver from the holster of a dead soldier on the ledge, thumbed back the hammer, and triggered one shot left, another right. Then he bounded up and over the stockade wall, dropping

79

down the other side and landing on both feet, bending his knees to absorb the shock with his boots.

The girl screamed once more—a thin, vibrating rattle dwindling into the distance. The Trailsman turned to see the brave running north through the ankle-high grass, a gray shadow in the dying light, the girl flopping down his back, red hair flying.

Horseback Indians galloped in circles as rifles spoke from the stockade wall. The attackers seemed to be withdrawing, loping away or sprinting off toward the horses they'd left when they'd stormed the fort. Several lay humped in the grass, bleeding, while a couple crawled, groaning or wailing their death songs.

Fargo leaped over a dying warrior and stretched his legs in the direction of the brave retreating with Valeria. A couple of arrows stitched the air around him, bullets from the fort whistling over his head, but he continued pushing off his heels, raising his knees high, scissoring his arms, bounding after the brave.

He crested a low hump of ground tufted with young chokecherry shrubs, and felt his gut knot with frustration. About forty yards ahead, a brave on a cream horse led a tall paint toward the brave carrying Valeria. Both braves whooped and shrieked victoriously as the first brave threw Valeria over the paint's back.

"Skye!" the girl screamed again.

Fargo cursed, his breath rattling in and out of his laboring lungs, and increased his speed. The thunder of hooves suddenly grew out of nowhere to flank him, horses snorting and blowing. Fargo kept his gaze straight ahead, on the brave now mounting the paint behind Valeria.

He closed the gap to within ten yards.

The brave with Valeria turned his head toward Fargo, grinning maniacally while Valeria, lying belly down across the horse before him, kicked and thrashed.

Fargo threw himself forward, preparing to bolt from his heels to throw the brave from the paint's back. But before he could set his feet, a horse's head smacked his right shoulder blade.

Suddenly, he was airborne, twisting and pivoting. The ground came up to smack him hard between the shoulders, the back of his head feeling as though it had just been cleaved by a war ax. He slid through the grass, the ground raking him, tearing at his buckskins and making his spurs ring.

As the horse that had rammed him continued past, more hooves thundered, making the ground shake. Fargo lifted his head, blinking the stars from his eyes.

A zebra dun closed on him, blocking out the dull green sky and the first kindling stars. The brave on the zebra's back screamed, mouth and eyes wide, as he stretched a nocked arrow back behind his right ear, aiming at Fargo.

The Trailsman threw himself belly down on the ground. At the same time, he heard the whistle of the arrow and felt the wind of the horse passing over him, a hoof nipping his calf.

The brave who'd just passed over him and the brave who'd sent him wheeling galloped off after the brave who'd nabbed Valeria, all three horses turning gradually west and disappearing into the thickening prairie shadows.

Fargo glanced ahead. Not two feet away, a painted arrow shaft angled up from the ground, its point buried in the short grass between a small sage shrub and a flat, lichen-mottled rock. The arrow was fletched with raven feathers, bespeaking the Raven Clan of the Blackfeet, a people Fargo had last seen in their customary stomping ground near the Milk River paralleling the Canadian border in northern Montana Territory.

Pain lanced the back of his head, driving deep into his shoulders and down his spine. Fargo let his head sag back against the ground, noting the dwindling of the rifle fire and of the hooves clomping around and behind him.

He was vaguely aware of time passing, then, as if in a waking dream, a man's deep-throated voice called his name. Spurs chinked. Prairie Dog Charley called again, his voice and spurs growing louder. There was a flapping sound, like a holster smacking a thigh. A bulky silhouette dropped down to Fargo's right, sheathed in the smell of sweat, tobacco, and gunpowder, and a thick hand clutched Fargo's arm.

Prairie Dog was breathless. "You still kickin', Skye?"

Fargo lifted his eyelids, which seemed weighted down by an unseen hand.

"I see you still got your hair, you son of a bitch!" said Prairie Dog, kneeling beside Fargo and whipping his head around cautiously. "How you've managed to keep that thick mane after all these years in Injun country, I'll never know!"

Fargo lifted his head slightly, wincing at the daggers of pain. "The girl," he croaked. "They got the major's daughter . . ."

"You think I'm deaf, blind, *and* stupid?" Prairie Dog gave a tug on Fargo's arm. "Let's get you back inside the stockade where the sawbones can tend that wooden mallet wabblin' around atop your shoulders."

"Don't need a sawbones," Fargo growled, rising clumsily, nearly tripping over his own feet as he stared after the fleeing Indians. "Have to get after the girl."

"You ain't gettin' after the girl tonight. Those savages'd love to pick us off in the dark."

Fargo cursed and let Prairie Dog lead him back toward the stockade. A few shots rose from inside the

82

wall—no doubt soldiers finishing off wounded Indians. The rolling terrain around Fargo and Prairie Dog was eerily silent in the aftermath of the raid, with here and there a dark body humping up above the grass or a riderless pony dropping its head to graze.

In the far distance, the fleeing raiders yowled like coyotes over fresh carrion.

"How many of our men bought it?" Fargo asked.

"Hard to tell. I'd say a dozen, maybe more. Good thing we had our best riflemen on the shooting ledge." Prairie Dog spat. "As soon as they got the girl, the whole bunch skedaddled. Almost like she was what they came for."

He and Fargo were twenty feet from the wall when the double doors shoved outward with a raspy rake of unoiled hinges, the door bottoms crunching cacti and sage and raising dust. Obviously, the doors on this side of the stockade were rarely used.

The silhouettes of a half dozen soldiers in various condition of dress jostled out, holding rifles high across their chests and swiveling their heads around nervously. The group opened to reveal two more men moving slowly behind them. One—an older gent with long gray hair in a ponytail falling over his shoulder and wearing a tattered red robe and slippers—held the other around the waist as they shuffled toward the Trailsman and Prairie Dog.

"Fargo, is that you?" the major barked, his voice pinched with pain. "Don't tell me those savages got away with my daughter!"

As the soldiers fanned out in front of the wall, crouching over the fallen Indians and prodding the bodies with their rifles, Fargo and Prairie Dog drew up before the major and the gray-haired gent, doubtless the camp medico.

Ten or so inches of an arrow shaft sprouted from

the major's left shoulder, which meant the point was protruding from the man's back. He must have taken off his tunic before the attack; he now wore only a white, long-sleeve undershirt and suspenders. The blood had formed a dark stain down the front of his shirt to his cartridge belt. His red hair was mussed about his hatless head. Howard's right hand was wrapped around the shaft where it met his shoulder, blood glistening in the ambient light, and he staggered on his booted feet as though drunk.

"They got her, Major."

"Christ!" Howard winced and groaned, stumbling back against the doctor. "I told her not to go traipsing about the grounds after dark."

Fargo felt his face heat with chagrin. He thought he saw Prairie Dog glance at him knowingly, but maybe it was only his imagination.

"Corporal!" the major barked toward one of the soldiers milling about the dead Indians beyond the stockade wall. "Form a contingent immediately! I want those savages run down before—!"

"Now, Major," Prairie Dog broke in, still holding one of the Trailsman's arms. "You'd only be sending those men to their graves. We're badly outnumbered out here, and any contingent you sent out wouldn't see midnight."

"For the love of Christ, Robert, come to your senses!" the doctor added in a slight German accent. "That's just what the Indians are hoping you'll do, so they can *slaughter* some more of us. You'll have to wait till morning. Now, let's get you over to the infirmary so I can remove that arrow before you *bleed* to death!"

Shifting his weight from one foot to the other, the major turned to Fargo, a helpless, confused, beseeching cast to his gaze.

"Prairie Dog and I'll head out at first light," Fargo said. "The smaller the pursuit party, the better. We'll get her, bring her back, and *then* we'll go after Lieutenant Duke."

The major nodded dully. He let the doctor half turn him toward the fort, then stopped and glanced skeptically at the Trailsman. "Have you any idea what she was doing around the stables, Fargo? Not a very likely place to find my daughter at such a time . . ."

Fargo flicked his gaze toward Prairie Dog, then back to Howard, and hiked a shoulder. "I reckon she's fond of horses, Major."

Major Howard squinted one eye.

"Come on, Robert," the doctor said, tugging on the man's good arm.

Howard let the doctor lead him back through the open gate. The Trailsman turned to see Prairie Dog regarding him severely. "Child, you're gonna get yourself shot one of these days, with that overused organ of yours up the wrong girl's honeypot!"

More sporadic gunfire sounded from behind the stockade wall as Fargo and Prairie Dog tramped after the major, the Trailsman muttering, "We should all retire so nobly."

Just inside the stockade, he and Prairie Dog stopped and looked around at the dead Indians and soldiers lying in the shadows behind the hay barns and remount stables. Small groups of living soldiers crouched around the wounded while others hauled men toward the infirmary on stretchers.

Torches cast a guttering radiance from the direction of the parade ground and officers' quarters. Occasional horse whinnies broke the eerie quiet while coyotes yammered in the hills surrounding the fort, no doubt frenzied by the smell of blood.

"If they'd used fire arrows, this coulda been a whole

lot worse," Prairie Dog remarked. "I reckon I'll help tend the wounded and haul off the dead savages. You best get to bed, Skye. We'll get started at first light."

As Prairie Dog moved forward, Fargo touched the scout's arm. "I ain't gonna get any sleep, Dog. How 'bout you?"

Prairie Dog squinted an eye at him, his face partially concealed by shadows, light from the torches dancing dully in his deep-set eyes. His voice had a dread tone. "What's on your mind?"

"Let's get after them."

"You're addlepated, child. Like I told the major, they'd swarm us, ambush us, scalp us, and boil up our privates for dog feed!"

"Not you an' me." Fargo smiled grimly. "Remember the *Montana Rojo* in 'fifty-six?"

"We got lucky."

"We rescued those girls from the Comanch by moving the way *they* moved—slowly, quietly, staying low, then swinging wide to creep up *in front* of 'em."

Prairie Dog snickered as he scrubbed his beard with his sleeve. "Surprised the shit out of 'em, we did!" His snicker died suddenly and he stared off toward the dancing torchlight before turning back to Fargo, the light now bright in his eyes. "How's your head?"

"It needs air."

"Well, it's liable to get plenty of air!" Prairie Dog cursed, ran his hand across his own scarred, hairless pate, then set his hat back on his head and began striding off between the hay barns. "I'll fetch Brunhilda and meet you back here in twenty minutes!"

He muttered darkly as he ambled off in the shadows.

10

Fargo fetched his gear from the sutler's store while the sutler and his half-breed wife hauled from their porch a dead warrior whom the woman had nearly blown in two with her husband's old blunderbuss.

In the stable, the Trailsman saddled the pinto, stuffed his saddlebags with the provisions Valeria had given him, then headed off to the stockade's north gate. He waited only five minutes for Prairie Dog Charley to pull up on a stout blue roan rigged with the old scout's fancy Schuetzen target rifle.

"The major was under the doc's knife, so I told Lieutenant Ryan we were headin' out." Prairie Dog chuckled woefully. "The lieutenant's a might rattled, I fear. He told me he wasn't expectin' to see me, you, the girl, or *anyone outside the fort* ever again, but that he'd pray for our deliverance from those screaming heathens!"

Fargo turned the pinto straight north, intending to swing wide of the retreating Indians before heading west, paralleling their path. "A good man in a pinch, the lieutenant."

He and Prairie Dog kept to the coulees and valleys as they headed straight north of the fort, spying no

Indians or white men or even much wildlife except an occasional meadowlark or finch flitting about the chokecherry and juneberry scrub lining the creeks and streams.

What they did find were several burned out settlers' homesteads, charred bodies and stock animals strewn about the corrals, cabins, and mine diggings, as though they'd been flung by some angry god from outer space and pincushioned with feathered arrows. A couple of young prospectors had been decapitated, their rotting heads placed on their dugout cabin's rough-hewn table, facing the door—a grisly, blackly humorous welcome to visitors.

The two scouts continued north as the sun rose, then swung west along the intermittently dry watercourse of Tongue Creek, where Fargo had once hunted buffalo and nearly been scalped by Cree. At noon, they paused on the shoulder of a low butte and stared into a hollow in which a dugout cabin nestled with a weathered privy and a cottonwood corral.

The place looked abandoned, though no dead littered the tawny, dry grass. A weathered canoe was tipped against the side of the cabin, nearly buried in wild rye.

In the middle of the yard, a windmill turned lazily. Water trickled from a log pipe into the stone tank shaded by a gnarled box elder.

"They must've pulled out when they got wind of the Injun trouble," remarked Prairie Dog.

Fargo didn't say anything. He stared at the windmill, listened to the tinny gurgle of the water dropping into the tank. Their horses hadn't had water since dawn, and his and Prairie Dog's canteens were half empty.

Prairie Dog read Fargo's mind. "Should we ride down?"

"Looks clear to me," Fargo said, "but, then, those were the last words of many a dead man."

Prairie Dog lifted his hat, ran a hand across his scarred pate. "And many a *hairless* man." Rising in his saddle, he looked around, grunting. "Why don't I ride down from that east bluff, and you come in from the west? If there's anybody down there, one of us oughta savvy him. Though, like I done told you, a post can pick up more sound than my right ear."

"Then listen hard with your left," Fargo grumbled, reining the pinto right and walking out along the hill's sloping shoulder.

Keeping one eye on the cabin below and another on the grassy terrain before him—the water might have drawn any number and any breed of visitors— Fargo circled around to the west, then dropped down off the hill, angling into the yard.

The ground between the cabin and the windmill, still soft from a recent rain, indicated no recent traffic. Still, he held the pinto to a shambling walk as, hand on his .44, he approached the clattering windmill and the gnarled box elder whose leaves whispered in the slight breeze.

There was the smell of old manure from the corral on the other side of the windmill, damp earth, and the green, salty reek of the water.

When Fargo was fifteen feet from the box elder, something moved in the corner of his right eye. He sawed back sharply on the pinto's reins and whipped his head around.

Three white-tailed does angled up a grassy bluff about two hundred yards south, beyond a stand of cottonwoods and the rocky bed of Tongue Creek. Their hooves thumped softly, crackling the dry grass. A spotted fawn followed from a distance, bleating like a worried rabbit.

The Trailsman grabbed his rifle, threw himself out of his saddle, and hit the ground flat-footed. At the same time, Prairie Dog's voice rose in the west, "Pull out, Fargo!"

Sensing it was too late to gallop out of the yard without getting blown out of his saddle, Fargo slapped the pinto's butt with his rifle stock and bolted toward the stone stock tank. A bullet clipped the lip of the tank with a whining spang, flinging rock shards, then slapped the water.

From the direction of the cottonwoods, a rifle cracked.

Fargo hit the ground beneath the tank, swiped his hat from his head, and edged a look around the tank. More guns barked, black powder smoke puffing up around the cottonwood trunks. Another bullet plunked into the stock tank, and then another chewed a dogget from a corral slat.

Fargo lifted his Henry and fired two quick rounds through the corral slats into the cottonwoods, one round tearing bark from a bole while another spanged off a rock in the riverbank beyond. He fired two more rounds at the smoke puffing amongst the branches, then bolted up and ran west along the corral, crouching and squeezing the Henry in both hands, wincing as several rifle shots tore more wood from the slats to his left.

He dove behind a springhouse, fired three rounds from the west side of the house, hearing a clipped yell from the trees, then continued running southwest, dodging sporadic bullets and tracing a weaving course amongst brush-sheathed boulders. He turned around another dilapidated springhouse nestled between low bluffs, and headed directly toward the cottonwoods in the east from which the gunfire was picking up, most shots apparently directed at someone other than Fargo.

Hooves thundered in the brush before him. Fargo crouched behind a rock pile at the edge of a small irrigated garden. Prairie Dog's blue roan bounded up out of the riverbed, shaking its head, trailing its reins, and snorting frantically. It galloped over a hummock and disappeared into the thick brush behind and to Fargo's right, stirrups flapping like wings.

Fargo cursed and rammed a fresh shell into his Henry's breech. He'd run two steps toward the cottonwoods when a couple more shots crackled. Behind the broadest cottonwood, a man screamed horrifically. Brush thrashed under running feet, and labored breaths rose.

A man bounded out of the trees, angling southwest along the riverbed—a slender young Indian, long hair and trade beads flapping down his back. Grasping a rifle in one hand, he wore a long deerskin shirt and knee-high moccasins. He stopped, wheeled suddenly, and, holding the rifle by its barrel, slung it back into the cottonwoods with an enraged epithet which, roughly translated from the Assiniboine, meant "Fuck you!"

He wheeled again, grunting painfully as he continued running southwest, limping on his right leg.

In the cottonwoods, a pistol popped. The slug barked off a rock a few yards in front of the fleeing brave.

The pistol popped again, and the brave's head snapped to one side. He cursed again but continued running.

Footfalls sounded from the cottonwoods. Fargo shuttled his gaze from the fleeing brave to the trees just as Prairie Dog emerged from the grove.

Fargo blinked as the stocky, paunchy man in buckskins and knee-high, stovepipe boots bounded over the rocks and sage clumps like a man half his age. Prairie Dog leaped a boulder, losing his leather hat, then stopped and extended the bulky Colt Patterson in his right hand.

"Dry-gulchin' red bastard!" Prairie Dog shouted, canting his head to stare down the revolver's barrel.

The Patterson roared, black smoke puffing around the barrel. Climbing the ridge on the other side of the creek bed, grabbing at the shrubs for purchase, the brave stopped suddenly.

He lifted his head and grabbed his back while clutching an ironwood branch with his left hand. Slowly, he released the branch, fell straight back down the hill, and rolled through the shrubs before piling up, unmoving, at the base.

Fargo felt his lip lift a smile as he dragged his gaze back to Prairie Dog. Staring at the dead brave, the stocky scout dropped the smoking Colt to his side and started forward.

"That all of 'em?" Fargo yelled.

Prairie Dog stopped and turned. "Sure as shit." Then he continued toward the dead brave.

Fargo whistled for his stallion as he walked over to where Prairie Dog stood at the base of the ridge, kicking the brave over to make sure he was dead. "Those three whelps musta been headin' for the water when they seen us with our hats aimed in the same direction," said the old scout. "The other two are about his age, maybe a little older."

"Nice shootin'," Fargo said, pulling the loading tube out of the Henry's breech to replace the spent cartridges. "Here I was startin' to think you were too damn deaf and stove-up to fight Injuns."

Prairie Dog grinned proudly, squinting one eye. "Shit, what the hell I need you for? I done took out them first two from the hill with my sweet Brunhilda." He laughed. "Got one through an ear, the other through his brisket while you was dodgin' their bullets in the yard."

Prairie Dog looked around. "You seen my horse? Brunhilda's burp always spooks him."

"Went thataway," Fargo said, jerking a thumb over his shoulder. "Where's Brunhilda?"

"Left her coolin' back in the trees."

Fargo turned to his own stallion glaring at the dead Indian from several yards behind the Trailsman. Fargo looked around cautiously as he shoved his Henry into the saddle boot. "Let's fill our canteens and get the hell out of here. Where there's three wolves . . ."

"Yeah, I know," Prairie Dog said, starting back toward the cottonwoods. "The pack ain't far away."

Apparently, the pack was farther away than they'd thought. After filling their canteens and continuing southwest, Fargo and Prairie Dog had no more Indian contact for the rest of the day.

That night, camping in a dry creek bed with no fire, and washing biscuits, venison, and cold beans down with water, they heard nothing but occasional bats and nighthawks, a lone wolf in the northern buttes.

Around three o'clock, Fargo heard the keening mutter and the light tread of a mountain lion passing through the ravine. After his skirmishes with the Blackfeet and Assiniboine, he gave the panther little more concern than he would a garden snake. He merely recrossed his ankles, pulled his hat brim lower, and rejoined the raucously snoring Prairie Dog in slumber land.

They came upon fresh Indian tracks about an hour after sunup the next morning—a good twenty or thirty unshod horses moving west at a ground-chewing clip. Two hours later, they crossed the far westward curve of Squaw Creek, and halted their horses. They stared northwest along the ancient, curving riverbed they'd been following since early morning.

Ahead, a great deciduous forest sprawled for a good two or three miles in the north and south, stretching before them like a lumpy, jade quilt to the far western horizon. Above the quilt, the black smoke of a dozen fires lofted skyward.

"Well, I'll be a monkey's uncle," Prairie Dog said, his voice hushed and nervous. He hipped around in his saddle to rake his cautious gaze in a complete circle around them. "I think we might've just found what we're lookin' for, Mr. Trailsman, sir."

Fargo had fished his spyglass out of his saddlebags, and directed it toward the trees, lips stretched back from his teeth as he adjusted the focus. "The Box Elder buttes," he muttered. "Twenty square miles of woods and buttes, and right in the center, Cottonwood Creek meets up with the north fork of the Squaw in a deep ravine."

He turned to spit a weed seed from his lips, then returned his eyes to the glass. "With all those buttes and trees, it's a right good place for warring Injuns to hole up unseen."

"Yeah, they got 'em a natural buffer against interlopers, that's for damn sure."

"It's too hard a place to get into twice. Let's try to find the girl and follow through with our original assignment."

Prairie Dog looked around again, scrubbed sweat from his bearded jaw. "How you wanna wrestle this hog? Them woods and buttes are probably peppered with pickets. And Miss Valeria—if she's here—ain't gonna be unattended."

Fargo scanned the woods for another minute, then reduced the glass and slipped it back into his saddlebags. "Let's mosey a half mile back the way we came, picket our horses where they won't be found. We'll wait for sunset, then move through the woods on foot."

Prairie Dog snorted. "You mean, just walk into their camp, say, 'Pardon me, boys, but I'm here to shoot the crazy fuckin' white man poundin' the drum for this here powwow. Oh, yeah, and could you tell me what ya done with the white girl you nabbed?' "

"Well, shit," Fargo said with feigned exasperation, reining the pinto around. "Why ask if you already know the answer?"

11

The Trailsman and Prairie Dog Charley tied their horses to saplings in a box canyon offshoot of Squaw Creek. They removed their boots and socks, then grabbed their rifles and extra ammo, and crept back along the shallow watercourse toward the woods.

They moved with practiced stealth, heads moving constantly as they scanned the terrain around them for Indians, noses sniffing the breeze for the wild, greasy odor of a native. When they were a hundred yards from the woods, they discovered an Indian picket perched on a southern bluff, hair blowing in the breeze as he stared straight west, a bow beside him, a war lance angled across his outstretched thighs.

Fargo and Prairie Dog ran crouching along a ravine bottom, Prairie Dog narrowly escaping the strike of a coiled sand rattler. They paused at the edge of the woods—mostly ash and box elders with a few giant cottonwoods churning in the evening breeze, blackbirds cawing amongst the branches—then glanced carefully around once more before turning into the trees.

The woods had appeared much denser from a distance. Inside the sprawling copse, the trees were spaced ten and sometimes twenty feet apart, with deadfall humped on the ground or leaning like crutches against standing trunks. Occasional willows clumped with chokecherries or burr oak snags.

There were several winding deer paths, many marked with fresh horse prints. Fargo and Prairie Dog each chose a paralleling path and moved westward through the woods, about fifty feet apart, putting one bare foot down in front of the other, making as little noise as a coup-counting redskin.

The air was rife with the smell of loam and decaying leaves, the wild-rose smell of chokecherries. Dim light shafted through the canopy to speckle the forest floor.

They'd pushed a hundred yards into the woods when something thrashed wildly in a hawthorn snag ahead and right of Fargo. Both men froze, crouching, hearts pounding, bringing their rifles to bear. Fargo threw his left hand up as a white-tailed buck sprang from a hawthorn snag and bounded off to the north, leaping over fallen trees, its knotted, sprawling rack trimming low branches with riflelike cracks.

The men shared a glance as the crunching hooffalls dwindled into the distance. Adjusting the grips on their rifles, they continued forward at roughly the speed of a racing turtle.

They moved at the same pace for over an hour, until the trees thinned. Ahead, the smoke from several fires thickened, scented with the smell of burning wood and roasting meat. A low din sounded, like that of a town heard from a distance, drowned occasionally by dog barks and the screams of playing children.

Fargo and Prairie Dog dropped to their hands and knees and crawled to where the forest stopped abruptly at the lip of a broad, deep canyon. A few feet back from the lip, the men stopped and, shielded by rocks, brown wheatgrass, and shrubs, stared into the broad sweep of the canyon cut by two streams.

One of the streams, only twenty or thirty yards wide, curved through the canyon directly below Fargo and Prairie Dog, flowing from west to east. The other meandered in from the southwestern side of the canyon, joining the first about a half mile right of the men's position atop the ridge.

The Indian village nestled inside the broad L shaped by the two streams, amongst cottonwoods, willows, and musk grass—a good forty or fifty lodges of tanned buffalo skin, all doors facing east and fronted by smoldering cook fires. Women in doeskin dresses tended the fires or scraped hides stretched between stakes, while naked children frolicked and dogs milled. A stout woman in a calico dress and deerskin leggings chased one mongrel from a bucket of what appeared to be buffalo brains with a bone-handled broom, her voice rising in raucous admonishment while the dog yelped and ran.

Fargo's gaze followed the dog to the sandy flat bordering the confluence of the two streams. Near the gently churning water, a pit had been dug and lined with red, green, and white colored stones. A couple of braves, clad only in loincloths, were clearing the pit of charred wood, throwing the logs into the stream, while another split logs with a hatchet and stone mallet nearby.

The braves near the fire pit were the only males within sight. The others were no doubt napping in their lodges, waiting for the women to cook their supper, or off hunting or rampaging. A hundred yards southeast of the camp, where the prairie rose away from the streams, a good fifty mustangs milled in a broad brush corral. They grazed or trotted friskily, whipping their manes in the breeze.

There was no sign of Valeria. But then, the Trailsman knew that locating her amongst a group this size would be at least half as hard as rescuing her.

Fargo glanced at Prairie Dog, who scanned the village through his spyglass. "That pit down there near the confluence is for ceremonial bonfires, or I miss my guess."

"Maybe a powwow tonight."

Prairie Dog patted his sleek, brass-chased Schuetzen as though it were a beloved pet. "If Duke's involved, he'll be well within range of my sweet Brunhilda."

Fargo fished his own spyglass out of his boot, directed it toward the village. "If we don't spy the girl soon, I'll sneak down after good dark, try to pull her out of there. Most of the Injuns'll no doubt be attending the festivities around the fire pit."

"You'll be lookin' for a needle in a haystack, Skye. If Miss Valeria's even still alive."

Fargo shrugged, but anxiety over the girl nagged him.

"What about Lieutenant Duke?"

Fargo stared through the glass, slowly sweeping the village from left to right and back again. "We'll pass on him till we get the girl." He lowered the glass and turned to Prairie Dog, pensive. He kept his voice low. "Give me a good hour after sundown. Then, if you get a shot at Duke, take it."

He raised the glass again and continued scrutinizing the village. He stared through the glass until his vision blurred and his head ached from the strain. Slowly, the sun sank into the western prairie, splashing a painter's palette of colors into the sky. Then the colors faded and the first stars kindled.

In the village below, torches flickered to life, and shadows began scuttling about the lodges. A drum sounded with the rhythm of a slowly beating heart.

A few minutes later, a soft glow appeared in the fire pit below the ridge and on the far side of the stream. Soon the flames were leaping six and seven feet in the air, sparks rising and dying as they drifted toward the stars.

Fargo heard the crackling and snapping of the burning logs above the drum's beat and the stream's murmur against the ridge. Warm air rife with the smell of burning ash and box elder pushed against his face.

"Show time," Prairie Dog said, keeping his bald head low, adjusting his elbows in the dry grass.

Fargo lifted the spyglass, shifted the magnified spear of vision around the fire. The silhouettes of feathered warriors circled the fire pit. Some danced wildly, throwing their hands in the air with warlike yelps, others merely shuffling, hop-skipping, or taking short, buoyant strides while shaking rattles or spears.

When thirty or so dancing braves and older, potbellied warriors had circled the fire, women and girls of all ages traced another circle behind them, some dancing to the rattles and drums, some merely walking solemnly and holding the hands of children. The women were dressed in beaded doeskin and moccasins, some with their hair pinned up while others let it hang down their backs, the bear grease glistening in the umber firelight.

When the women had completed their circle behind the men, the drumbeats increased and grew louder. An old man—tall and broad but weathered like an old cottonwood, shoulders bowed, and wearing a warbonnet with streaming eagle plumes—lifted his chin and began singing softly. A buffalo robe hanging off his shoulders, and a necklace of his enemies' teeth hanging around his neck, he gradually increased the volume until his keening voice echoed shrilly around the canyon, and distant coyotes yammered in answer.

This was Iron Shirt, Chief of the Coyote Band of the Assiniboine—a wily, cunning old war chief with whom Fargo had skirmished on the plains between the Missouri and Souris Rivers, barely escaping with his life each time.

Fargo dropped his spyglass to his chin and glanced at Prairie Dog. "Looks like most of the village has gathered for the hoedown. Duke must have convinced them they're invincible—that's why there aren't many pickets. You stay here. I'm gonna go down and look for—"

"Hold on," Prairie Dog growled as he stared through his own glass at the fire.

Fargo directed his glass toward the east side of the dancing, billowing flames. A tall, white-skinned figure entered the sphere of firelight.

The man's pale blond hair hung to his shoulders, held back from his face with a rawhide thong encircling his forehead. His face was painted like that of a warring savage, the eyes deep-sunk and shadowed, broad chest bare and massed with tattoos of many shapes and colors including bright red serpents surrounded by ravens rising from his ribs. He wore a calico loincloth and fringed deerskin breeches, which hung to just above his knees. A dagger jutted from a beaded sheath on his right hip.

As Lieutenant Duke approached the fire, he raised his arms straight out from his chest, slowly flexing his knees. His singing rose to meet that of Iron Shirt, the otherworldly keening of both men becoming one demonic dirge.

The coyotes yammered even more shrilly, a bizarre accompaniment to the cacophony rising from the village.

The hair on the back of Fargo's neck pricked.

A shadow moved behind Duke. Fargo shifted the spyglass slightly, and adjusted the focus.

"Sweet Christ," Prairie Dog muttered to Fargo's right.

Two braves stepped into the firelight. They carried between them a long platform bedecked with deer or antelope skins. On the skins sprawled a pale, naked girl, her slender arms hanging down from the platform's edge. Valeria's distinctive hair—long and thick and the bright red of a prairie sunset—hung down from the end.

Valeria Howard.

The braves positioned Valeria beside the fire, to Duke's left, and lowered the platform to their shoulders. The fire glistened off Valeria's pale, curving body, the full globes of her naked breasts casting oval shadows across her belly. She lifted one knee, dropped it across the opposite thigh, and wagged her head back and forth, face pinched. She'd been drugged.

Fargo's heart quickened. He continued staring at Duke and Valeria through the spyglass as he snarled, "Dog, grab Brunhilda and draw a bead on that son of a bitch!"

"What about . . . ?"

Prairie Dog's voice trailed off as, through his own spyglass, Fargo watched Lieutenant Duke lower his hand to the sheath on his right hip, and draw the bone-handled dagger. The man lifted the dagger toward the fire and continued singing along with Iron Shirt, slowly flexing his knees, staring into the flames with the countenance of a man mesmerized by his own madness.

"Shit!" Prairie Dog lowered the spyglass and grabbed the Schuetzen. He inspected the muzzle-loader, made sure he had a patch seated on the nipple, then snugged his cheek up to the rifle's sleek stock, and drew back the hammer.

Fargo stared through the spyglass as Duke sang on one side of the fire, Iron Shirt on the other, both raising their hands high above their heads, the war chief's eagle plumes dancing in the fire wind. The others—women as well as men—sang softly, dancing in place.

Duke's trembling dagger glittered in the firelight. Slowly, he lowered the blade to the flames, as if to sterilize it. The singing grew louder. Quickly, Duke removed it, swung around toward the girl.

Fargo turned away from the spyglass. "*Shoot* the son of a bitch, *Dog!*"

"I told you my eyesight ain't as good as it used to be," the old scout spat. "And it's even worse at *night!*"

Below, Duke flapped his arms slowly, and the braves lowered the skin-draped platform until Valeria lay writhing on the ground in front of the mad lieutenant. Duke dropped to his knees, raised the knife in both hands above his head as if in prayer, and sent a wolflike howl rising to the stars.

Despite himself, Fargo jerked with a start.

Duke lowered his left hand slowly, leaving the right one holding the dagger high in the air, the glinting, silver blade angled toward the girl struggling languidly upon the skins.

Fargo snapped, "Goddamnit, Prairie—!"

To his right, the Schuetzen belched and flashed, the stench of burnt powder instantly filling the air. Below, a half second after the rifle's bellow, Lieutenant Duke's right arm jerked forward. At the same time, one of the two braves before him twisted around and back, grabbing his side with both hands and showing his teeth through a snarl.

Fargo steadied the spyglass as Duke fell forward over Valeria, dropping his knife, then twisting around to glare in the direction from which the shot had come, eyes bright with fury. All at once, the Indians dancing around the fire stopped and turned in the same direction, their singing transforming into a cacophony of angry snarls and exclamations.

An enraged voice rose in English, *"Attackers!"* Duke translated the shout, and instantly the crowd began scattering, the men dashing northward along the stream, heading for the bluff, the women and children fleeing toward the lodges.

Fargo lowered the glass and glared at Prairie Dog. "Nice shot!"

"It *was* a pretty good shot for these old eyes, ya damn ingrate." Prairie Dog stared down the bluff, at the surging black mass sprinting toward the river, the fleetest braves already splashing into the water. "But what the hell we gonna do now?"

Fargo cursed and looked back toward the fire. Valeria lay sprawled atop the animal skins. Duke knelt on one knee beside her, clutching his right arm as he glared toward the bluff.

Fargo cursed again as he dropped his spyglass into his boot well and grabbed his rifle. He and Prairie Dog might have spared the girl for the moment, but, doing so, they'd pretty well blown their own lamps while doing nothing for Valeria's future. To try to get around behind the approaching horde of raging Indians would be sure suicide.

And, to top it off, Duke was still alive . . .

"Well," Fargo said, on one knee as he stared down the bluff at the Indians yowling and crossing the stream, his steady voice belying his frustration, "I reckon we'd better run."

Down the slope before him, the Indians grunted and

yowled, loosing rocks and gravel as they scrambled up the bluff toward the interlopers. Clutching the Schuetzen, Prairie Dog scrambled to his feet and bolted into the trees behind Fargo.

"Skye, old son, I like how you think!"

12

Fargo squeezed off three rounds over the lip of the ridge, hearing a couple of grunts and enraged screams amongst the Indians approaching from below, then turned and followed Prairie Dog further into the woods. In spite of the inky tree columns and low-hanging branches, he ran hard, overtaking Prairie Dog in about seventy yards.

"Keep going!" Fargo growled. "I'm gonna circle around, see if I can sneak the girl outta the village!"

Prairie Dog took several more leaping strides through the woods. "But, hell, I won't make it, neither, so I reckon I'll see ya on the other side!"

"I'll see ya back at the *fort*!"

Fargo swung right into the trees, his keen night vision picking out deadfalls, which he hopscotched, ducking under branches, tracing a wide angle down hill and back toward the stream. He bolted through a juneberry thicket then stopped, listening.

Behind, branches and shrubs cracked under running feet, and the rasps of labored breaths rose.

Fargo ducked behind the thicket and edged a look back the way he'd come. Two jostling shadows ran toward him, starlight dancing on spear heads and on bone talismans hanging around the braves' necks.

Fargo snapped the rifle to his shoulder, triggered a shot. The Henry's bark shattered the heavy silence, and the brave on the left screamed. There was a heavy, crunching thud as he hit the ground and rolled.

The brave on the right kept coming, screaming, starlight reflecting from his wide eyes as he bolted into the thicket, drawing his spear back behind his ear, preparing to throw.

Fargo shot him twice in the chest. As the dying brave drove the spear into the ground and continued half running and half falling, propelled downhill by his own momentum, the Trailsman ejected the spent shell and continued scrambling down the bluff's steep shoulder.

He stopped beside a sprawling box elder at the lip of the stream bank, and turned back toward the Indian village. He could see nothing but the willows and cottonwood saplings lining the stream. Up the hill behind him came the occasional distant whoop of a brave still on Prairie Dog's trail.

Taking his Henry in one hand, Fargo grabbed a stout root bowing out of the bank, and dropped down to the soft sand lining the riverbed. He plunged through the willows and straight into the water, which, in spite of the sweat basting his shirt to his back and soaking his beard, braced him with its chill.

On the other side, he climbed the bank, water sluicing off his buckskins. Slogging through the scrub willows and sage and knee-high wheatgrass, he angled back toward the village, which he couldn't see from this distance.

When the lodges became conical shadows against the stars, the fire glowing ahead and right, near the confluence of the streams, he moved forward quickly, crouching, keeping his head below the tops of the scrub willows. A dog barked somewhere to his left. Fargo hoped the beast was tied, or his position would be discovered in no time.

Continuing to steal through the scrub, ignoring the sting of prickly pear and hawthorn, he crept between several dark lodges, firewood piles, and stretched buffalo hides. Edgy, angry voices rose around him—men's as well as women's—and several times he changed his route to avoid braves lurking about, armed with rifles or nocked arrows.

He crabbed around a heap of split wood, and stopped. Thirty yards away lay the fire, which had diminished considerably since Prairie Dog's errant shot. Fargo had just begun to scan the ground around it for Valeria, when angry female voices sounded faintly on his left.

He swung the Henry around, heart thudding. The cackling harangues, muffled as though by buffalo hide, seemed to originate from a nearby lodge.

Fargo jogged toward the voices but dropped when two braves jogged toward him from the fire. When they'd disappeared in the darkness, he continued forward. He didn't stop again until he knelt beside the closed door of the lodge from which cackles, angry snarls, and Assiniboine epithets emanated. Inside, a girl was sobbing, and there was the smack of a strap on bare flesh.

Fargo cursed, looked around, and crawled on hands and knees to the lodge's painted deerskin door. He lifted an edge of the flap and peered into the shadows jostled by a fire in the lodge's center, the smell of buffalo hide and smoke nearly taking his breath away.

Two Indian women knelt in the shadows, on either side of a pale figure writhing upon a buffalo robe. One woman had her hand on the back of Valeria's neck, forcing the girl's head down hard against the robe, while another, who wore her silver-streaked brown hair in a long braid down her back, lashed a strip of rawhide against Valeria's bare bottom.

As Fargo pushed through the door and stood, aiming his Henry straight out from his right hip, the woman facing him gasped, rising and stumbling straight back toward the far side of the lodge. The other remained kneeling before Valeria but turned toward Fargo.

She was a crone with a wizened face spotted with warts, and slanted, evil eyes. She neither gasped nor started but regarded Fargo coolly, almost bemusedly.

Fargo wagged the Henry's barrel and warned the women in his rough Assiniboine to think twice about calling out, for he had no qualms about shooting ugly Indian wenches. He'd barely slung the insult before he realized the woman facing him from across the lodge was far from ugly.

No older than eighteen, if she was that, she was strikingly beautiful—her black hair long and thick and burnished by the leaping flames at her side. She wore a wolf cloak around her shoulders, and her eyes in her heart-shaped face, with its strong nose and well-bred jaw, were almond-shaped bits of obsidian flamed by the thick wings of her hair.

A true Indian princess if Fargo had ever seen one. The slight drop of her chin and the flicker in her eyes told him she'd read the appreciation in his gaze.

Neither she nor the crone said anything as Fargo moved forward, grabbed a skinning knife from an overturned gourd, and reached down to cut the hide strap tying Valeria's right hand to a stake above her head. Long red welts streaked her back and buttocks.

It wasn't until he'd freed her left hand that her eyes

snapped open, and she turned her head slightly, blinking as she stared up at him.

"Skye?" she said weakly.

"Shh." He waved his rifle back and forth between the princess and the crone. The princess kept her chin down, upper lip curled, lustrous black eyes squinted.

When he'd cut all the straps, he held the rifle on the two women with one hand while awkwardly pulling Valeria up with the other. Obviously, she was too drugged to walk, so he drew her naked body over his shoulder. Hand clamped across her thigh, her head hanging down his back, he rose, backed to the door, and repeated his warning to the Indian women about calling out.

They glared at him like dark statues.

Fargo turned, bolted through the lodge's door, and crouched as he glanced around quickly. He hadn't taken more than two strides back the way he'd come before the crone in the lodge began shrieking like a hyena in a bear trap and the girl began shouting out the door in her quick, guttural tongue that a tall white man was making off with the fire-headed whore.

Wishing he had shot them, Fargo broke into a run, meandering between the lodges humping darkly around him. He turned past a large meat rack when men's voices and the clatter of running feet rose ahead.

Wheeling, he sprinted toward the horse remuda, the girl groaning and grunting down his back. He tripped over a lodgepole brace, and fell forward, the girl rolling on the ground before him, sobbing and yowling his name accusingly.

Behind him and left, enraged voices and footfalls rose.

Fargo reached for Valeria. "Sorry." Grabbing her arm, he tossed her over his shoulder, scrambled back to his feet, and, holding the rifle in his left hand, sprinted forward again.

If he could nab a horse, they'd have a chance . . . but the yowls of pursuing braves trailed him like devils' screams.

As Fargo passed the last lodges at the camp's southern edge and bounded over the lip of a steep gully, a panting, growling dog shot toward him like a missile and, when he was halfway down the slope, clamped its jaws around Fargo's left ankle.

"Fuckin' mutt!" Fargo barked, his left boot flying out from beneath him. The girl flew out of his arms and a half second later they were both tumbling down the grassy slope, limbs tangled, rolling over and over.

The girl groaned as she rolled in the grass before him. When they hit the gully's brush-choked floor, he reached for the rifle that had hung up on a shrub.

He swung the Henry around, but before he could poke his finger through the trigger guard, he froze. While the snarling cur tugged on his pants cuff, three long-haired, bare-chested figures stared down at him, nocked arrows cocked back behind their ears, the sharp stone tips aimed at Fargo's head. The ash bows creaked like leather.

"Hold it!" a voice boomed on the ridge, in English. "I want him alive!"

Fargo stretched his gaze beyond the three braves slightly relaxing their bows before him. Two men stood on the gully's lip. One, pale skinned and blond haired. The other, just as tall but slightly stooped and wearing a plumed warbonnet and buffalo robe, a feathered tomahawk in his right hand.

"We'll kill him and the girl together, thus doubling the amusement of Kundra-May-Na-Tee . . . and doubling our power against the white-eyes!" With that, Lieutenant Duke raised his arm above his head, waved his hand, and danced in place, howling like a coyote, then wheeled and strode away.

Chief Iron Shirt descended the slope, eagle feathers shimmering in the firelight behind him, necklace teeth clattering softly on his chest. He pushed between the braves to squat before Fargo, the man's black eyes meeting the Trailsman's. Iron Shirt smiled, showing naked gums between his long eyeteeth, the creases in his long, haggard face deepening.

"Skye Fargo," he grunted. "The war gods told me you would come. They spoke to me the night I learned you killed my son, Blaze Face. They told me you would come, and I and the war god, Yem-seen, who speaks in the voice of Lieutenant Duke, would satisfy my desire for revenge."

"Skye!" Valeria cried as one of the braves grabbed her hair and jerked her to her knees.

Fargo lunged toward him, bounding off his heels. Before he knew what he was doing, he felt the brave's neck in his hands. The brave screamed a half second before his spine snapped.

Fargo let the body fall, and wheeled. In the corner of Fargo's right eye he saw Iron Shirt flick his hand toward him, starlight winking off the stone club in his fist. The back of Fargo's head went numb, and the last sensation he had was of falling back into the brush, staring up at the sky, and watching the stars wink out.

13

A voice called to the Trailsman, but he couldn't make out the words that seemed whispered to him from outer space. Lolling at the bottom of a deep, chill, black ocean, he heard little more than a slow, garbled murmur.

Then the ocean floor surged, and his head bounced up from the sandy bottom. Pain shot through his ears and deep into his shoulders.

The caller seemed to move closer, and Fargo could make out his name. His eyelids fluttered, light penetrated the black water, and he found himself staring up at a beautiful, dark-skinned, heart-shaped face framed in raven hair streaked with burnished copper.

The girl smiled, showing white, perfect teeth except for a single chipped one, before she turned away from him, throwing her arms wide and careening through the air. Her hair flew about her shoulders, streaked by dancing flames.

As the girl disappeared in the shadows around him, Fargo felt the ocean floor surge again. But it wasn't an ocean floor he lay upon.

Turning his head slightly and rolling his eyes around, he saw that he lay on a bed of trade blankets and buffalo robes. The ground vibrated beneath him with the rhythmic throbs of several drums beating like an enervated heart.

The walls of the stitched and painted buffalo-hide lodge glowed with the light of the fire within and several fires without. The glow was interrupted by the silhouette of the dancing girl—the beguilingly beautiful princess Fargo had seen earlier with the crone. Her shadow revolved about the walls like the specter of some bewitching, otherworldly goddess, hair flying, her arms flung out as though she were swimming through air.

She danced around him several times to the throbbing beat of the drums. It made Fargo's eyeballs and head ache to watch her, but he couldn't help himself.

In her deerskin smock, which was cut low at the neck and under her arms, so that he could see the half-moons of her light brown breasts when she turned sideways, the nipples jostling against the deerskin as she danced, she seemed a creature from another universe. She seemed at once a woman and a child—sinister and frightening yet rife with primordial sexuality.

A necklace of light blue beads clattered softly around her neck. Her legs and feet were bare. When she twirled, the smock rose above her thighs to reveal her well-turned legs and smooth, round bottom.

The drums grew louder, but their rhythm slowed. She stopped before Fargo, stared down at him, her thick hair obscuring her eyes like a giant raven's wing. As the drumbeats grew suddenly faster and louder once again, she crossed her arms and lifted the smock above her head, tossing it aside to reveal her slender yet voluptuous body in all its naked splendor.

Her brown, pear-shaped breasts rose and fell sharply, the hard nipples distended.

In broken English she said huskily, "You who killed

my brother are a brave warrior." She rubbed her flat belly in a circular motion. "You, before you die, shall fill me with a warrior just as fearless and strong, and he, our son, will fight against you and your people. Such is the wish of the war gods."

The drumbeats raced for a time, and a man's singing rose amidst the cacophony, dying suddenly when the drumbeats slowed once again to the rhythm of a fast-beating heart.

The girl dropped to a knee, pulled the trade blanket off of Fargo. He looked down at himself. He was as naked as she was, his fully erect shaft angling back toward his belly.

"Christ," he muttered.

The situation was as bizarre and disorienting as any he'd ever been in. He'd eaten peyote a few times with the desert tribes, and, such was the beguiling influence of the girl and the firelight and his aching, swimming head and uncontrollable lust, that he felt as though he'd eaten a few now.

Was he really about to be *studded* to this girl?

The girl turned, dipped three fingers into a wooden bowl on a small log table, then turned to Fargo with the pale dollop of what smelled like bear grease on the tips of her three fingers. She closed her hand, lightly coating the palm, before wrapping her fingers around his cock.

Fargo stiffened as though at the prick of a sharp knife, and groaned. Her hand was smooth and warm, the grease slightly cooler. Slowly, she smeared the bear grease onto the swollen head, then began working it up and down the thick, throbbing shaft, the grease crackling and snapping as she worked.

"Does that feel good, white man?" she asked softly, her voice almost inaudible above the beating of the drums.

Fargo had to admit to the keenness of the girl's talent but, wincing against the sweet torture of her slowly pumping hand, he said only, "Christ."

She chuckled throatily and lowered her head to lightly nibble his balls, then moved up to his chest.

As her hair tickled him, she slid her breasts across his shaft, sending even more violent shockwaves of desire through his loins. She slid her breasts slowly around on him, the grease on his member crackling, her buttonlike nipples raking him sweetly.

Fargo's heart skipped several beats before continuing its rhythm, which had somehow been synchronized to that of the drums outside.

He was surprised to find that his hands weren't tied. Duke and Iron Shirt must be confident that the girl's charms were enticing enough to keep Fargo from snapping her pretty neck.

He considered it, but killing her would only get him killed all the more quickly. The silhouettes of two braves in fur capes and wolf heads shone through the lodge wall, on either side of the lodge's flap. They were guarding the door—ready sentinels with spears in their fists.

Fargo raised his hands to the girl's delicate shoulders, ran them down her thin arms as she groaned and squirmed around on his chest. She leaped up suddenly, straddling him, pressing her knees to his ribs, scuttling forward.

Arching her back and propping herself on her arms, she raised her bottom and slid her silky nest around on his shaft. The bear grease and her own fluids blended, crackling, as the fire snapped and popped, sending sparks toward the lodge's black smoke hole.

The girl's head hovered over Fargo, her chin up, eyes squeezed shut. She groaned and grunted, waggling her upturned ass and jerking her shoulders—a wild, half-crazed bitch in the grip of an undeniable, elemental desire.

Her love nest slid down over Fargo like a hot, wet glove fresh from the warming rack of a stoked oven.

The Trailsman sucked a sharp breath, tipping his head back, setting his teeth against the exquisite torture. She rose slowly up, dropped slowly down, groaning and sighing, tossing her head, her rich hair sliding across her shoulders. He closed his eyes and pinched her nipples, kneaded the grease into her breasts.

Outside, the drums thumped. The fires danced across the curving buffalo-hide walls, shunting bizarrely shaped shadows. A man sang softly—Fargo recognized the primitive, beseeching strains of Iron Shirt. A rattle shook.

The girl's knees dug into Fargo's sides, and she increased her rhythm, rising and falling more quickly, her sighs turning to squeals, her fingers raking the hard slabs of his pectorals. In seconds, she was raising and lowering her ass so quickly that she became a ragged brown blur in the air above and before him.

"Mmmmhhh!" Her grunts were like a panther's death spasms. "Uhnnn-*nah*!"

Over and over she repeated the cries as she bounced up and down on her knees, which gripped and dug into his ribs like a vise. The firelight played over her slender, bouncing body, the brown skin smooth as bone beneath his caressing hands. Her pink-tipped orbs bounced and swayed in blurs of frenzied motion beneath the clacking necklace.

"Ach-ah-*eeeeee*!" she chortled, as, with one final, violent thrust, she dug all ten fingers into his chest and threw her head back on her shoulders, shuddering as though she'd been struck by lightning.

The Trailsman clamped his jaws together as the girl's spasms gripped him. His own passion leaped to its climax, his seed firing straight up into the girl's heat.

He lifted his head, clutched her thighs with both hands, and ground his heels into the robes as he bucked up against her, spending himself. Exhausted, he lowered his head, closed his eyes, and let his exhaustion wash over him.

The drums ceased. Iron Shirt's singing faded.

The girl climbed off him, panting, flinging her hair back over her head, and padded off. He heard a rattle of cookware and the murmur of poured liquid.

His nose caught the scent of warm mint, and then her voice was a throaty whisper in his left ear. "Drink."

Head still reeling from the previous beating and the torrid sex, Fargo opened his eyes. The girl knelt beside him, offering a small wooden bowl. From the murky liquid inside, swirling steam wafted the heady aroma of fresh mint.

Thirsty, but too weary and disoriented to ask for water, he lifted his head, sipped at the bowl that the girl held to his lips. The minty fluid slid down his throat easily. He took several deep gulps, his body craving the sustenance.

He'd barely taken the last sip before his head grew heavy as a smithy's forge. The shadow and light-swept lodge pivoted sharply, and a loud screech rose between his ears.

He clutched the bed beneath him, as though at the edges of a swamping canoe. As his head fell back against the robes, his lids dropped like fifty-pound seed bags over his eyes, and downy white birds wafted across the purple gelatinous murk that had become his brain.

The birds winged through his skull for a long time, lulling him into a sleep nearly as deep as death. It was his own name that called him back as the ocean floor once again surged beneath him.

Recognizing the voice, he swam up from unconsciousness, hearing the birds' final muffled cries and wing beats, and opened his eyes. Wincing at a pain spasm, he found himself reclining against a naked, sand-peppered thigh. He was outside, on the ground, and staring up at the pretty, pale countenance—framed by mussed, sand-streaked, fire red hair—of Valeria Howard.

Frowning down at him, raking her hands through his hair, she exclaimed in a trembling voice, "Skye, you're alive!" She ran her hands across his face as though she were blind. "Oh, God, what did they *do* to you?"

Fargo glanced down at the ten half-moon-shaped cuts in his chest, and remembered the mauling he'd taken from the princess. He rose onto his butt, found that his wrists were bound with braided rawhide. His ankles were bound, as well, with an additional length connecting his ankles to a cottonwood post embedded firmly in the ground a few feet away. He and Valeria were naked, scraped, sand-caked, sunburned, and tied like dogs.

He cursed, yanked on the lanyard binding his ankles to the pole. Feeling as though he were still locked in the belly of a bizarre dream, his head still swimming from the braining, the tea, and the sex, he looked around.

The sun was angling westward in a cloud-spotted sky, which meant it was early afternoon. He must have been out here since last night. The buffalo-hide lodges rose above the willows in the south, smoke rising and floating between the lodge poles. In the north, the confluence of the two streams gurgled and rushed softly, while birds flitted in the brush lining the banks.

Only thirty yards west lay the cold, gray ashes of the fire pit.

Valeria sat back against the pole they were bound to, arms covering her breasts, knees raised. The sun and mosquitoes had splotched her otherwise smooth face. Her hair was tangled about her head.

She looked at once indignant, enraged, and terrified. "I thought you were dead." Her eyes dropped to the cuts on his chest. "What on earth did they do to you, Skye?"

Fargo felt his face warm with chagrin as he glanced away from her. "Some things are just too awful to talk about."

The brush along the river snapped. He turned toward it, ducked quickly as a rock careened over his head to bounce across the sand behind him.

The boy who'd thrown it—maybe six or seven years old and wearing only a loincloth but armed with a slingshot—threw his head back, pointing at Fargo as he laughed. The other two boys making their way out of the shrubs behind him laughed, as well. The three broke into runs as they headed for the village, cackling and chortling.

Fargo picked up a stone and slung it after them.

"They've been doing that all day," Valeria said hatefully. "The children come by and throw things. The dogs bark and growl. The braves make lewd gestures. An old woman came out and rapped me with a willow switch. I don't understand how you slept through all that."

"Well, I had a long night."

"I'm so scared. The braves have been gathering wood for another fire." Valeria's voice trembled as she turned her eyes to the fire pit, on the other side of which fresh willow and cottonwood branches were heaped. "What're we going to do?"

Fargo pulled at the leather lanyard binding him to the pole. There was no give whatever, and the expert knots were small and taut as sutures.

He inspected the braided rawhide binding his wrists. Those knots, too, would be impossible to untie, impossible to cut without a knife.

Clarifying rage burning through him, Fargo flung his wrists apart, the rawhide snapping taut and cutting into the chafed skin. If he didn't think of a way out of here soon, he and Valeria both would no doubt be sacrificed to the Assiniboine war gods, under the sharp knife of demented Lieutenant Duke, and to the ethereal singing of Iron Shirt.

Fargo exhaled slowly and peered toward the dun hills rising beyond the stream, where Prairie Dog Charley had no doubt met a slow, bloody end last night.

"What're we gonna do?" Fargo mused through a long sigh. "Good question."

14

Skye Fargo was not a man to give up easily, but after trying several times to loosen both his rawhide bonds and Valeria's, and receiving nothing for his efforts but broken, bloody fingernails, he threw in the cards.

He'd never be able to break the stout cottonwood post to which he and the girl were tied, but he gave it a couple of furious attempts . . . receiving little for *that* effort but a sore back and neck and adding more misery to his throbbing head.

The Indians only watched and laughed, a couple warriors wandering up to point out Fargo's and the girl's privates. One grabbed her breast, then sprung away, laughing, as she lunged to slap him. A stocky, middle-aged warrior who seemed to enjoy impressing the younger braves, came up and urinated on the post that Fargo was trying to pry out of the ground. Laughing and tucking himself back into his loincloth, he walked away, muttering to the others about dressing for the ceremony.

Fargo slumped down beside Valeria, on a dry side of the post, and propped his elbows on his naked knees. The girl hung her head and sobbed, which she'd been doing for the past few hours. Fargo didn't try to comfort her. She'd seen the wood the braves had gathered and chopped and seen, too, the post they'd erected in the middle of the fire pit. She'd read enough stories of Indian atrocities to know what the post was for.

She and the Trailsman were not to be stabbed or run through with war spears. They were to be burned at the stake, naked as the day they were born.

He turned to the boys tossing the chopped wood around the base of the stake, then glanced at the sky. The sun was nearly down, deep shadows bleeding out from the hills and knolls. The water gurgled beyond the cattails and willows.

He was still staring in silent frustration at the brush along the stream when, just after sundown and during the kindling of the first stars in the east, a drum began throbbing somewhere on the far side of the village.

The girl started.

Fargo turned to see five braves walking toward him through the willows, their purple shadows raking the sage and buck brush clumps. Three were bare-chested while one wore a tunic of bobcat hide with several emblems painted on it. Their eyes were dark, faces expressionless. The man in the tunic carried a wide-bladed, bone-handled knife down low in his right hand, while one of the others carried a spear. The other three fixed bows to arrow strings, angling the bow tips threateningly toward Fargo and Valeria.

Fargo stared hard at the approaching braves but directed his words at the girl. "Don't show fear. They don't respect fear, only bravery."

"Does it really matter at this point?"

"Just do as I tell you, damnit. It'll go worse if you show sign of weakness. And, if you see an opportunity, run to the river and swim for your life."

"What about you?"

"I'll put in a good word for you with the war gods."

"Thanks."

"Don't mention it."

The approaching braves spread out in a semicircle around Fargo and Valeria. The one in the tunic, the oldest of the five, gestured for the two captives to move back away from the pole.

When his orders had been obeyed, he stepped forward, crouched, and chopped through the two cords connecting Fargo and Valeria to the cottonwood post. As the man straightened, Fargo eyed the knife in his hand. If he could somehow grab it and chop the leather strap binding Valeria's feet, he might give the girl a chance, however slim, to live.

The Indian followed Fargo's gaze to the knife in his hand, and smiled. He stepped back, grinned conspiratorially at the other braves flanking him, then turned back to Fargo, open challenge in his eyes. He extended the knife toward the Trailsman in his open palm, as though daring him to grab it.

The Indian then closed his hand about the knife handle, swung his arm down to his right side, and snapped it up. The knife careened about six feet over his head, turning end over end once before falling. Falling, it turned end over end twice more before the handle dropped back into the Indian's extended hand.

The Indian stared with wide-eyed mockery at Fargo, then grinned broadly, his flat cheeks dimpling. He cut his eyes toward the other braves, who chuckled.

Fargo laughed.

The laugh died on his lips as he lunged off his bound feet, throwing himself up and forward and chopping his bound fists down against the hand in which the Indian lightly grasped the knife. The brave gave a startled grunt and stumbled straight back as the knife hit the ground in front of his moccasins.

Before the other braves realized what had happened, Fargo grabbed the knife, then twisted around and sprang toward Valeria, diving toward her feet. With a single chop, he cut her ankles free.

"Run!" he shouted, as an arrow parted his hair and sliced into the ground behind him. *"Head for the stream!"*

He quickly chopped through the ties binding his own ankles, and straightened. An iron-bladed hatchet careened toward him at the end of a naked brown arm. Fargo ducked. The hatchet whistled over his head, blowing his sand-crusted hair.

Instinctively, he thrust the knife forward and up.

The Indian grunted sharply, and warm blood gushed over the Trailsman's right fist. Before he could pull the knife out, an arm snaked around his neck, drawing his head up as it tightened, pinching off his wind and blood, and making his head feel like an overfilled balloon. Each heartbeat felt like a hammer smashed across his brain plate.

As the Indian drew him back and down, he glimpsed Valeria running off to his left, toward the confluence of the two streams. One of the other braves was close on her heels, yowling as he dove, wrapping his arms around her feet, tripping her. She fell face-first in the brush, screaming.

Fargo dug his fingers under the arm of the brave strangling him. Seeing two other braves standing before him, arrows aimed at his face from two feet away, their faces pinched with silent fury, he opened his hands, turned them palm out in surrender.

The arm of the brave in the wolf-hide tunic slackened around Fargo's neck. One of the braves before him slitted his eyes, drew his aimed arrow back slightly.

The brave under Fargo asked the enraged brave, in

Assiniboine, if he would cheat the war gods' fire. Both warriors quickly lowered their arrows. The arm drew away from Fargo's neck, and the warrior in the wolf-hide tunic shoved him aside, rising and cursing in Assiniboine as he turned away from Fargo to the brave kneeling with the knife still embedded in his belly.

Calling the brave a girlish fool to be killed so easily, he reached down, pulled the knife from the brave's bloody gut. The brave threw his head back screaming, then fell straight back in the brush, thrashing. The warrior in the wolf-hide tunic extended the blood-drenched knife toward Fargo, wagged it up and down from a good five feet away, the mockery in his eyes replaced by wary respect.

Swallowing, trying to reopen his pinched, battered windpipe, Fargo straightened. Behind him, the girl sobbed and kicked against her captor, who dragged her by the hair through the brush, and tossed her down at Fargo's bare feet.

"Pick up your whore, white man," the warrior in the wolf-hide tunic ordered, grabbing Fargo's own Henry repeater off the ground, racking a fresh shell in the chamber, and aiming at Fargo's head. "Then over to the fire pit, where the war gods will enjoy seeing you dance together in flames."

Fargo reached down to where the girl sobbed, legs curled, her head buried in her arms. He grabbed one of her arms, gently drew her up beside him. She no longer tried to cover herself, and her bare breasts, sandy and dusty and spotted with grass seeds, jostled and swayed.

"Sorry," he grumbled as the braves flanked him from several cautious feet away.

She rose up on her tiptoes, kissed his lips, then turned to let him guide her toward the fire pit. "Thanks for trying, Skye."

Thanks for nothing, Fargo thought, as the Indians prodded him and the girl into the fire pit, turning their backs to the post. She would have been better off dying by Lieutenant Duke's knife than dying with him here tonight—slowly, by fire.

Valeria didn't seem to feel the same way, however. Fargo was amazed at how stoically she suddenly seemed to accept her fate.

As three warriors held the rifle and the bows on her and Fargo, the fourth bound them to the cottonwood pole with coiled rope. The rope was wrapped around their bodies and the pole between them from their shoulders to their ankles, drawn so taut that Fargo could take only shallow breaths.

The brave had no sooner knotted the rope around the base of the pole than a distant drum began to throb, and the Indians—old and young warriors, old and young squaws, children, and their dogs—began to filter onto the ceremonial grounds from the lodges. A handful of warriors rode in on sweat-lathered mustangs, dismounting and howling victoriously, as though fresh from a raid, joining the milling throng around the fire pit.

When they'd all gathered, dancing and singing, dogs barking and running with the children, a torch shone in the direction of the village, a bright, flickering light in the thickening darkness.

"Here we go," Fargo muttered.

The girl, out of sight behind him, on the other side of the pole, said, "Skye?"

"Still here."

"I would never have admitted this under ordinary circumstances, but . . ." Her voice trailed off uncertainly, dwindling beneath the din of the surrounding revelers.

"If it's a long confession, you'd best hurry."

"I love you." Valeria paused as the drum's beat grew louder, the torch grew brighter before Fargo. "I fell in love with you the moment I first laid eyes on you in Mandan."

"Figured as much."

In the corner of his right eye, Fargo saw her head turn sideways to the pole. Rage trilled in her voice. "You *bastard*! That's all you have to say?"

"Right changeable, aren't we?"

A rock careened out of the milling shadows of the crowd to his left, struck the pole just above his and Valeria's heads. A little boy, naked and holding a short, feathered lance, ran into the crowd, grinning devilishly.

"You little urchin!" Valeria cried. "Can't you people raise your children any better than that?"

The drum grew louder. Fargo stared straight ahead as a tall, blond silhouette and a stooped, stocky figure approached through the willows, flanked by braves carrying torches, the hide lodges lifting conical shadows behind them.

Lieutenant Duke, wearing nothing but a loincloth, a red bandage on his upper right arm, moccasins, and a hide thong around his head, grabbed a torch from a brave, held it aloft, his eyes fluttering, trancelike, as he sang in the ethereal, ceremonial tones of the Assiniboine. His tattooed breasts were hideously scarred from the sun dance ceremony.

Light, sparking embers, and shadows danced bizarrely.

Beside Duke, clad in warbonnet and buffalo robe, the regal Iron Shirt thumped the drum in his hands, taking little march-dancing steps, rising on the balls of his feet, as he and Duke drew up to the ring of branches mounded about the cottonwood post.

The pair stopped in front of the ring of wood piled haphazardly around the stake, about ten feet in front of Fargo. Both men locked gazes with the Trailsman. Iron Shirt's tobacco brown eyes were glazed with solemn religious fervor. Lieutenant Duke's blue eyes, above small lightning bolts of chokecherry die on the nubs of his sunburned cheeks, owned as much zeal as Iron Shirt's, but the white man's zeal was sheathed in raw, blind insanity.

The man should have been locked up in the funny house. Instead, here he was, having thrown in with one of the most powerful war chiefs on the Great Plains, exacerbating Iron Shirt's hatred for the whites. In addition, he'd convinced Iron Shirt that he had a direct link to the Assiniboine war gods, and could lead him in war.

As Duke and Iron Shirt sang, Duke's features garish in the light as he waved the torch, the Trailsman spied the princess he'd coupled with last night, standing about ten feet to Lieutenant Duke's right.

Beside her stood the gray-haired crone who had whipped Valeria's bare bottom. On the other side of the crone stood another, heartbreakingly pretty Indian girl—obviously the princess's sister though slightly taller, her belly rounded with child.

Duke's child, judging how the girl stared at the crazed white man with gooey, proprietary admiration.

The princess who'd shared Fargo's robes last night held a fox cloak around her shoulders, her hair glistening in the firelight. She must have sensed his stare. She turned toward him, gazed at him obliquely, then quickly turned to the two men leading the ceremony, drawing her cloak tighter about her shoulders and shaking her head haughtily.

Fargo turned back to Duke and Iron Shirt still singing and waving the torch and thumping the drum while the throng sang and danced and the children laughed and the dogs barked.

Fargo clamped his jaws and shouted, "Just get on with it, you long-winded sonso'bitches!"

As if to comply with the Trailsman's wishes, Duke moved to his right, Fargo's left, and touched his torch to the dry wood. The brittle brush instantly caught fire, glowing, sparking, and smoking.

The wind pushed the smoke toward the stake, making Fargo's eyes sting. Valeria coughed and swung her head from side to side.

Still singing, Duke walked past Fargo, to Fargo's right, and touched the torch to the brush at the west end of the ring. He danced back toward Iron Shirt, singing, dancing, and waving the torch, his blue eyes flashing the religious zeal of the unequivocally mad, and reclaimed his position beside Iron Shirt.

As the flames began leaping up from the wood on either side of Fargo, the Trailsman coughed and blinked his burning eyes. The heat pushed against him, sweat gushing from his pores and dribbling down his chest and arms. He heard Valeria coughing behind him, felt her fighting against her stays.

He glanced at Iron Shirt. The old chief held Fargo's gaze with an enraged one of his own, lifting his right fist, clenching it furiously.

The war chief's expression tightened, and the anger in his eyes was replaced by a vague surprise. Through the undulating heat waves, Fargo saw a black circle in the middle of the old man's chest.

The Trailsman blinked. Had the circle been there before—some talisman or war marking?

As though wondering the same thing, Iron Shirt glanced down, stumbling straight back and dropping his drum at his feet. He looked up again, brown eyes glazing, and the report of a high-caliber rifle echoed above the crowd's din.

A fraction of a second later, there rose the buoyant bugling of a cavalry horn.

15

As the peal of the bugle cut across the night, evoking a collective grunt from the Indian revelers, Lieutenant Duke turned to Iron Shirt. The chief raised his hands toward the bullet hole in his chest, and dropped to his knees.

The crone standing between the two pretty princesses to Fargo's left began shrieking like a witch with wolves on her heels. At the same time, rifles popped above the fierce attack cadence of the growing bugle cry.

The gunfire rose from the buttes above the river, as well as from the flats straight east, and the Indians—women, children, old warriors, and young braves—began scattering south and west. Several of the armed braves loosed war cries, looking around wildly while raising their feathered lances. A half dozen others gathered around Iron Shirt now lying belly down in front of the fire.

Coughing and blinking against the smoke and leaping flames around him, Fargo turned to see Lieutenant Duke running toward the lodges, shouting orders for the others to grab their weapons and hold back the blue army hordes.

Behind Fargo, Valeria gasped and groaned at the wafting smoke and leaping flames.

Rifles and pistols popped from the direction of the river. Hooves thudded in the east. Several braves threw war lances or loosed arrows; several more dropped as slugs plunked into their chests or bellies. The others, taken by surprise, and unprepared for battle, followed the brunt of the crowd south and west through the willows and cottonwoods, fleeing enemy fire.

As one lone, stubborn brave loosed an arrow eastward before clutching his neck and dropping, the hoof thumps rose from that direction, and a horseback rider appeared, galloping into the sphere of tossing firelight. The Trailsman's saddled pinto followed the bearded, buckskin-clad rider, led by its reins, its tail high, eyes flashing.

Fargo blinked through the smoke and flames stabbing up in front of him as Prairie Dog Charley drew his dun to a halt before the fire and, tossing a brass bugle out of his hands, leaped out of the saddle like a kid half his age. He ran up to the fire, slitting his eyes in their doughy sockets, regarding the fire warily.

"Forget it!" Fargo shouted. "You'll never make it through the flames, Dog. Do us a favor and give us each a bullet!"

"I didn't go to all this trouble fer nuthin', Godblast it!"

Looking around, Prairie Dog grabbed a fallen lance and began thrusting it into the flames, shoveling aside the burning logs and branches. He leaped back as flames shot out at him, soot and sweat bathing his round, bearded face, then bolted forward once more to continue carving a path through the conflagration.

Flames leaped up around the Trailsman's bare legs, and he winced at the burn, the smoke now funneling up his nostrils like thick pepper, searing his eyes and lungs.

Behind him, Valeria coughed and sobbed. "Oh, God," she cried. "I'm *burning*!"

"Not if I have anything to say about it, honey!"

Prairie Dog threw down the lance, grabbed the big bowie off his left hip and, bellowing like a wild man, leaped through the slim corridor he'd carved in the dancing flames. Eyes slitted, coughing, he hacked at the rope coiled around the pole, starting at the top and working down.

When he'd cut through the bottommost coil, he yelled, "There!" and grabbed the girl's right arm. As he pulled her back through the corridor sheathed in flames, Fargo pushed away from the stake, ripping the severed ropes away from his body.

He turned to follow Prairie Dog and Valeria, but the flames closed the corridor, erasing Prairie Dog's buckskin-clad back. Peering left, he saw a slight break in the flames and, roaring like a lion about to lunge for freedom, dove through the thickening wall of fire and coiling black smoke.

He hit the ground outside the fire ring, worms of smoke curling up from his shoulders, feeling like a charred shank of venison, smelling the fetor of his own charred hair and eyebrows. He'd fallen just right of Iron Shirt's slumped form. Shaking his head and blinking the smoke from his watering eyes, he bounded up onto his heels and looked around.

To his left, Prairie Dog had dropped to a knee, extending his Colt revolver. Flames lanced from the barrel as the Colt barked and leaped in his hand. Amidst the willows, a shadow fell, but more braves were dancing around in the brush, no doubt having retrieved their rifles and bows.

Spying his own Henry repeater lying over the

slumped form of the warrior in the wolf-hide tunic, Fargo leaped forward, grabbed the rifle, and dodged an arrow that plunked into the fire behind him. He snapped the rifle to his shoulder and fired three times at the dancing shadows, one of which flew backward while the others scattered, howling.

Prairie Dog continued firing eastward as Fargo sprang toward him and the horses dancing on the other side of the fire. Valeria hunkered behind a willow, knees covering her breasts, hands clamped to her ears.

"Let's get the hell outta here!" Fargo grabbed Valeria and tossed her onto the Ovaro's back.

As he snapped up the sagging reins, Prairie Dog triggered a final shot and wheeled toward his own mount. "But I was just startin' to have fun!"

Fargo looked around as he swung up into the saddle, hearing another arrow whistle past him and evoking a shriek from the girl. "Where's your soldiers?"

"They lit out!" Prairie Dog bellowed, swinging heavily into his own saddle. "There was only four of 'em in the first place though we tried like hell to sound like a whole company!"

As Fargo reined the Ovaro into the brush lining the stream, holding the Henry in one hand and wincing as his bare balls ground against the saddle horn, he turned toward Prairie Dog galloping off the pinto's left flank. "Why the hell didn't you kill *Duke*, for chrissakes?"

Both horses plunged into the water as the warriors' enraged shrieks rose behind them, arrows slicing the air and tearing into the weeds. "I was aimin' fer Duke but pinked old Iron Shirt instead! I told ya—!"

"I know," Fargo yelled as the horses gained the opposite bank and angled toward a natural trough in the butte facing them, "your old eyes ain't worth shit in the dark!" He cursed loudly as a rifle barked in the direction of the villages, the slugs tearing into the weedy, chalky butte face.

"You ungrateful nub!" the old scout bellowed, his tack squawking as he followed Fargo up the butte. "I shoulda just rescued the girl and left you to burn, damn your nekkid hide!"

Valeria clutched the Trailsman snugly around the waist as the Ovaro lunged up and over the lip of the butte. Blowing, it continued over the top and lunged down the other side, the whistling of the arrows and hammering of the rifles dying behind them, the enraged calls of the Indians fading on the night breeze.

Fargo was so relieved to be free of the Indians' fire that he didn't even feel ridiculous, straddling the pinto buck naked, the Henry repeater resting across his saddle bows, the naked girl clinging to his back. The cool night breeze felt keenly refreshing against his sunburned, fire-scorched skin.

He nor the girl nor Prairie Dog said anything as they galloped north of the Indians' camp, tracing a serpentine route through the buttes. The Indians had seemingly been so startled by Prairie Dog's attack that they were slow to mount their horses and form a pursuit party.

Fargo didn't hear or see anyone behind them, but he didn't take any chances. He didn't slow the pinto until he'd slipped into a dry creek bed carved between high, grassy buttes stippled with burr oaks, sage, and occasional cedars, with here and there a rocky shelf protruding from a hill shoulder. He didn't stop the horse until he'd followed an offshooting gully into a narrow, rocky defile cloaked by aspens, pines, and large, mossy boulders.

He dropped to the ground, the sage and tough

grama grass feeling like broken glass under the scorched soles of his feet. He turned as Prairie Dog drew his own horse up behind the Ovaro, the old scout crouched slightly in his saddle.

"We'll rest here, then continue north," Fargo said, reaching up to grab Valeria around the waist. Too weary for modesty, she did nothing to cover herself. Her full, pale breasts were soot-streaked. "I wanna get good and clear of the camp before I circle back for Lieutenant Duke."

Fargo set the girl on the ground, then reached for the bedroll tied behind his saddle. Behind him, Prairie Dog remained mounted, leaning forward, leather hat tipped low over his forehead. "You two are gonna have to ride on without me."

The scout's gravelly voice was tight, and he was breathing hard. He snaked his right arm across his belly, trying feebly to reach around behind his back. He gave up the motion and reached behind with his left hand instead, lifting his head abruptly and showing his large, yellowing teeth through a sharp wince. "I reckon I turned pincushion for one of those red savages' arrows."

Fargo cursed. "Sit tight."

He jerked the blankets of his bedroll free of their leather ties, quickly wrapped them over the girl's shoulders, and hurried back to Prairie Dog. A fletched arrow protruded from the scout's back, just beneath his left shoulder blade. Blood stained his buckskin tunic, forming a long, glistening swath straight down from the shaft. The head was probably buried about five inches deep in Prairie Dog's back.

Fargo reached up, wrapped his right hand around the scout's broad upper arm. "You stopped one, all right. Get down here—let's have a look."

"Shit!" Prairie Dog groused as he climbed slowly out of the saddle, half leaning on the Trailsman.

Fargo led him over to a low rocky shelf flanked by a small piñon, and eased him into a sitting position. Prairie Dog looked Fargo up and down and chuckled.

"Sorry, Skye, but it's kinda hard to take you serious without any clothes on. Why don't you at least try to hide that well-used dong of yourn. Shit, them red savages even hide their private parts!"

"Shut your trap," Fargo said, pulling the man slightly forward so he could inspect his back.

The girl moved between the horses, holding the blanket tight about her shoulders and frowning down at Prairie Dog. "Does it hurt bad, Mr. Charley?"

"Hell." Prairie Dog gritted his teeth as he leaned over his knees. "I been stung worse by horse fli— achh! Goddamnit, Skye, what the hell you tryin' to do to me?"

Fargo had nudged the arrow slightly with his right index finger, to see how firmly the tip was set. "Horse flies, huh?" He made a face. "Looks to me like that point is resting against a rib. No way to push it through *or* pull it out."

"Ah, Lordy—no, I reckon not." Prairie Dog rocked forward, then back. "You're gonna have to leave me while you two go on north. Don't worry—I got a bottle of whiskey and my sweet Brunhilda."

"I'm not gonna leave you, you old bastard."

Fargo walked over to his saddlebags, withdrew a whiskey bottle and tossed it to the old scout, who caught it one-handed, wincing, then grinned and popped the cork. He began tipping the neck to his mouth, glanced at the girl sheepishly, stopped, and offered the bottle to her.

When she shook her head, staring down at him with a pained, concerned expression, he chuckled, relieved, and threw back a shot. He raised the bottle to check the level. "With the bottle I got in my own pouches, that'll do me till tomorrow, anyways. You go on, Skye. Those Injuns'll be scourin' this country in no time . . . 'specially since I ventilated old Iron Shirt."

Fargo had no intention of leaving his old friend here alone to die. He fished a bundle of spare clothes from his saddlebags and, untying the leather thong knotted around the bundle, turned to Prairie Dog, frowning. "What about those shooters in your attack party?"

"They're what's left of a lost patrol out of Fort William. They'd been *seventeen* men, and now they're only *four*—a sergeant, a corporal, and two privates. A tough, canny crew if I ever seen one. I come upon 'em night before last, when I outrun those Injuns foggin' our asses.

"They were holed up in an old prospector's sod shanty. Didn't have a single horse amongst 'em, and they were shot up somethin' awful. One had even lost his hand. But they still had the bark on, and some ammunition, and they all wanted a go at those Injuns—even if it was a *last* one.

"We all agreed to split up after our so-called attack. The soldier boys—them that made it—are probably circling back to their soddy. I told 'em I'd send help when I could find help my ownself."

"You had me fooled." Fargo had pulled on a pair of long underwear and was stepping into his spare buckskin breeches. "I thought for sure you were a whole company."

"I reckon my buglin' helped." Prairie Dog tossed back another drink. "I was a bugle boy for C company back in Illinois, when we was fightin' the . . ."

He let his voice trail off, lowering the bottle and lifting his head to peer along the black ridge rising before him. Fargo had heard the distant thump of a half dozen sets of horse hooves and the muffled, guttural strains of Indian talk. The hooffalls grew slightly louder in the west before gradually dwindling as the Indians, skirting the canyon, continued north.

Then there was only the sigh of the wind in the brush along the ridges and the solitary cry of a nighthawk.

"They'll be kickin' around here all night," Prairie Dog growled. "You two best split the wind, head back to the fort, and don't stop till you get there."

Fargo continued dressing. The only garments for which he didn't have spares were his hat and boots. He'd have to go bareheaded, but he found a threadbare set of old moccasins at the bottom of one of his saddle pouches.

He pulled them on, then walked over to Prairie Dog, drew the man's bowie knife from its sheath, and grabbed the bottle from the scout's hand.

"Hey, what the hell . . . ?"

"Just need a little to sterilize your knife."

"My knife? What for?"

Fargo splashed whiskey on both sides of the razor-edged bowie. "That arrow has to come out of there, or you'll bleed dry."

Groaning, Prairie Dog told Fargo he'd wait for a sawbones, but the old scout knew from experience that he wouldn't make it through the night with the arrow in his back. He removed his hat and sagged belly down into a thick patch of grama grass along the base of the rocky ridge. After another long pull from the bottle, he let Fargo cut his shirt away from the shaft.

Valeria knelt near the scout's head, watching Fargo begin cutting through the bloody skin along the protruding arrow, an expression of horror and fascination on her regal, disheveled features. Behind her, the horses, tied to shrubs, stood tensely, nickering no doubt at the distant sounds of the tracking Indians and the nearer smell of blood.

Prairie Dog had had arrows dug out of his hide before. Biting down on a bullet while Fargo worked, cutting down along the shaft to dislodge the steel tip wedged between two ribs, he grunted and cursed, apologizing to the girl for his language.

Valeria crouched over the scout's back, wincing as Fargo removed the bloody shaft from the wound, and tossed it into the brush.

Panting, Prairie Dog turned his head to one side. "Goddamn, Skye—pardon my blue tongue, little lady— but I do believe you enjoyed that!"

"Ain't done yet," Fargo grunted, holding up a needle and length of catgut thread from his sewing kit, threading the needle by the light of the rising quarter moon.

He'd just finished sewing up the old scout's wound and splashing whiskey over the sutures when Valeria said suddenly, "Listen!"

Fargo corked the whiskey bottle and froze.

Hooves thudded only a few yards back along the gully.

16

Fargo motioned for Valeria to remain silent as he rose from beside Prairie Dog and slipped his Henry from its saddle boot. Quietly levering a shell, he ran a settling hand down the Ovaro's long, white-striped snout—both the pinto and Prairie Dog's blue roan had been trained not to start in tense situations—and walked back along the narrow defile.

Near the intersecting ravine, he stopped as guttural voices rose softly, and an unshod hoof clacked off a rock. Fargo cat-footed forward and pressed his back to the rocky wall of the defile a few feet back from the intersecting ravine, half hidden from the ravine by brush and a scraggly cedar.

He held the Henry straight up and down before him, breathed shallowly, listening as the horses moved slowly toward him, hooves clomping, a couple of the Indians muttering quietly. When the horses were close enough to smell, Fargo tensed, pressed his back harder against the rock wall, and squeezed the Henry.

Bulky, black shapes moved on his left. A horse blew. Another shook its head. Men breathed.

Fargo didn't turn his head to look directly at the intersection of the two defiles, but he knew the Indians were staring down the one he was in. He felt the warriors' eyes penetrating the darkness and hoped like hell he blended with the rock wall and the cedar.

Someone clucked, and hooves thumped, growing louder until a horse's head moved into the narrow defile from Fargo's left. The rider drew back on the rope halter, stopping the horse about ten feet in front of the Trailsman. The horse was a steel dust with a small blue Z within an orange sun painted on its neck.

The horse stared straight down the narrow defile, toward Prairie Dog and Valeria about fifty feet beyond. The dun twitched its ears and lifted its snout, working its nose.

Fargo's back tightened. Would the horse sense the other two horses, smell the blood that Prairie Dog had lost?

Still pressing his back against the rock wall, Fargo looked up through the branches of the gnarled piñon. The tall, light-skinned man sitting the saddle was wearing Fargo's high-crowned, broad-brimmed hat, blond hair falling to his shoulders, his chest bare except for a thin, deerhide vest.

Fargo's pistol belt and Colt .44 were wrapped around the man's waist and loincloth. His moccasined foot was so close that Fargo could have swatted it with his rifle barrel.

If the Trailsman had been alone, he would have shot the mad lieutenant out of his saddle, but there were at least a half dozen braves sitting horses in the shadows behind Duke. Killing the self-proclaimed shaman would get not only Fargo's wick trimmed, but Valeria's and Prairie Dog's, as well.

Duke suddenly threw his head back and howled like a moon-crazed coyote. Fargo started, slamming the back of his head against the rock wall. The high yammer, so loud that it raked the Trailsman's eardrums, chased its own echo around the defile and set a couple of actual coyotes yammering in the northern distance.

The Indians behind the lieutenant grunted and muttered, amused. Duke's horse turned suddenly toward Fargo. The steel dust's eyes, meeting Fargo's, widened suddenly, showing the whites. Fargo began swinging the rifle barrel down and tightening his finger around the trigger.

One of the Indians behind Duke spoke loudly and fast, something about hearing movement on the opposite ridge.

Duke drew back on the horse's reins, clipping the horse's startled whinny, turning the animal away from Fargo and around toward the warriors. Duke and the Indians spoke too quickly for Fargo to follow, and then hooves clomped, tapering off back down the ravine.

Fargo sighed, the painfully taut muscles in the back of his neck relaxing. He took a couple of deep breaths, then tramped back along the defile to where Valeria knelt beside Prairie Dog, who lay belly down, one of the girl's blankets draped across his back. The man breathed steadily, deeply, moonlight reflected off his grizzled, bald pate and the single human tooth hanging from his right ear.

"Did they leave?" Valeria whispered.

Fargo nodded, staring down at Prairie Dog. "He's out?"

"Passed out right after you left."

Fargo turned to Prairie Dog's blue roan and unbuckled the latigo strap under the horse's belly. When he'd set the saddle, blanket, the scout's saddlebags, and rifle scabbard in the brush, he turned to Valeria. "Sit tight. Try to keep him comfortable. Build a small fire only if it turns cold and he gets overly chilled."

Holding the ends of the blanket across her chest,

Valeria stared up the Trailsman, frowning. "What're you going to do?"

"I'm going after Duke, and I'm going to kill the crazy son of a bitch if I can get a shot at him."

A thought dawning on him, he reached down and pulled the old scout's target rifle out of its scabbard. The Schuetzen was a better long-range shooter than Fargo's Henry repeater, and a long shot might be the only shot the Trailsman would get.

Holding the fine German rifle in one hand, he pulled the Henry from his own scabbard with the other, leaned it against a rock. "I'll leave that for Prairie Dog, though I hope like hell he doesn't have to use it."

He slid the Schuetzen into his own saddle boot, and glanced at Valeria. She was still staring up at him, her green eyes bright in the moonlight, her full lips parted slightly. Her breasts pushed against the trade blanket. Fargo moved to her, grabbed her brusquely, and kissed her.

"I'll be back."

"Be careful."

He swung onto the pinto and turned the horse down the dark, narrow cavity, heading for the main ravine.

Fargo picked up the Indians' trail on the northeast side of the gully. He also found the sign of a bobcat— a fresh track and warm scat—which was no doubt what the braves had heard and what had drawn them out of the ravine.

The Indians had continued northeast along the swelling prairie. Fargo followed slowly, keeping a close eye on their trail, which wasn't easy to follow in the dark and on the relatively hard, grassy ground.

Strips of terrain overgrazed by bison helped to show the tracks of the eight unshod ponies, as did a recent prairie burn. But when daylight streaked the eastern horizon and burnished several long, low clouds, he still hadn't overtaken the group but counted himself lucky not to have ridden into an ambush.

Lieutenant Duke and the braves obviously figured Fargo, Prairie Dog, and the girl were headed back toward Fort Clark and were hoping to cut them off. Rage at the invasion of their camp and at the killing of Iron Shirt must be driving them, because they sure as hell were tearing up the sod.

The sun had just separated from the eastern prairie and Fargo was climbing the long, low swell of a shale-capped dike, when the clap of gunfire broke the morning quiet. A prairie falcon, its wings coppered by the rising sun, swooped over Fargo's head and continued north, shrieking.

Several more quick, angry shots rose from straight ahead—a good mile or more away—and Fargo swung out of the saddle, wincing when his charred soles touched the prickly earth. Ground-hitching the pinto, he jogged to the lip of the dike, which faced east, and dropped to his knees behind a lone hawthorn shrub.

His keen eyes scanned the murky morning shadows beyond him, but he didn't spy movement until several more shots rang out, followed closely by a bizarre, victorious yowl—the crazed yammer of a madman.

Just beyond the next rise, similar to the one upon which Fargo lay, several shadows milled amongst the brush. A horse galloped straight south along the valley, buck-kicking and trailing its reins, its saddle hanging down over its ribs. Its terrified whinny rose shrilly, quickly absorbed by the vast, pale green sky.

Unable to see much from here, Fargo jogged back down the rise, mounted the Ovaro, and rode north, paralleling the crest of the long bluff before dropping over the bluff's north shoulder and into the valley below.

The distant gunfire ceased, replaced by the beseeching screams of a man in deep physical pain.

A narrow ravine twisted through the valley, angling along the base of another bluff standing between Fargo and Duke and his howling victim.

Leaving the Ovaro ground-tied in a cottonwood swale, Fargo grabbed Prairie Dog's Schuetzen from the saddle boot, wedged a second spare revolver—a .36 Colt—behind his cartridge belt, then dropped into the ravine. Keeping his head below the ravine's steep but shallow rim, he followed the dry watercourse's gravelly floor toward the rising screams punctuated by Duke's demonic yelps and howls.

When the screams seemed to be coming from his right, Fargo stopped and edged a look over the ravine's lip. Fifty yards away through the gray sage and bunchgrass tufts, several horseback braves milled, riding in broad circles around Lieutenant Duke who stood menacingly over a blue-clad man sprawled on the ground before him. Waving a bloody knife in the air, Duke howled. He bent down, his blond hair and the Trailsman's own hat dropping below Fargo's field of vision.

A man screamed shrilly—a long, hopeless cry of excruciating agony. *"No!"* he shouted. His voice cracked, and he sobbed, panting. "I don't . . . I don't know where they went, you crazy son of a *bitch*!"

The Trailsman leaned the Schuetzen against the side of the gully, the barrel extending far enough that Fargo could locate the gun easily if he needed it. Snakelike, he slithered up over the lip of the gully and crawled through the sage and bunchgrass, gritting his teeth, cocked .44 in his right hand.

"It's too bad you don't remember, you feeble white-eyes!" Lieutenant Duke shouted. "It is too bad you—nothing more than prairie vermin crawling out from your civilized white society—had the unfortunate gall to kill the bravest war chief who ever walked the plains and stalked the buffalo!"

A blade whispered through flesh. The soldier howled shrilly. "I didn't kill him, damn your hide. And you're as white as I am, you crazy bastard!"

Lifting his head from a clump of bunchgrass, Fargo glanced around at the horseback riders milling around him—seven painted braves on snorting mounts. Their attention was on the man staked out on the ground before Lieutenant Duke, whose back faced Fargo from twenty feet away.

Fargo stretched the cocked Colt straight out before him through the coarse blond grass, squinting one eye as he stared down the barrel. He planted his sites on Duke's back as the crazy lieutenant leaned down to swipe his blade once more across his staked, howling captive.

Suddenly, hooves thundered to Fargo's right. He turned quickly. A brave was bearing down on him atop a brown and white pinto. The brave shrieked, wide brown eyes glistening in the sunlight as he leaned over his horse's right shoulder, drawing a bow string taut, the nocked arrow aimed at Fargo.

Fargo jerked right, stumbling as he gained his feet. The arrow clattered off a rock to his left. He triggered the Colt then ducked as the horse galloped over him, wincing as a foreleg nipped his thigh.

When he glanced up again the brave was still somersaulting through the air to hit the ground on his head and shoulders, his neck snapping audibly to leave him quivering amidst the grama grass and pokeweed.

Behind the Trailsman rose a coyotelike yammer as

the other six braves loosed war whoops and gigged their horses toward Fargo, two bearing down with rifles, two with bows, another with a war lance painted the gray and blue stripes of the Coyote Clan.

Straight ahead of Fargo, Lieutenant Duke cocked his arm and tossed his bloodstained knife. Fargo leaned sideways, and the blade sliced across his upper arm—a long but shallow cut from which blood glistened instantly.

The Trailsman snapped up the .44 and fired at Duke, flinching as the war lance whistled past him. The mad lieutenant howled and clapped a hand to his ear, blood seeping between his fingers. Fargo whipped his gun around and blew the brave who'd just thrown the war lance out of his saddle with two shots through his breastbone.

The brave hadn't hit the ground before Fargo jerked suddenly, as though he'd been hit in the chest with a sledgehammer. An Indian galloping behind the brave he'd just killed screamed victoriously as his horse whipped on past Fargo, who glanced down to see a fletched shaft protruding from his left shoulder.

The Trailsman whipped around. The brave who'd fired the arrow reined his horse sharply with one hand while reaching into his quiver for another arrow.

Fargo emptied his Colt into the brave's neck and chest, then ducked several bullets slicing the air around him. He dropped the Colt and grabbed the spare .36 from behind his cartridge belt.

Suppressing the hot, stabbing pain of the arrow in his shoulder, he began pivoting on his hips and heels, picking out the three other targets surrounding him, the .36 belching and smoking in his clenched right fist—*pop, pop, pop-pop, pop!*—before the last three horses galloped off, riderless, reins bouncing along the ground behind them.

Staggering slightly, squinting through the wafting powder smoke, Fargo looked around.

Four braves lay silent and unmoving. A fifth was crawling feebly after the horses, head and hair hanging, blood painting a swath behind him. A sixth lay on his back, coughing between the somnolent notes of his death song.

The young soldier whom Duke had staked out, spread eagle to the sun, turned his shaggy head left and right and up and down, glancing around, terrified. His blue, yellow-striped uniform pants were threadbare. He wore no tunic, just a torn undershirt and one suspender. Blood glistened from the shallow cuts on his arms, thighs, and belly and from the cuts and bruises on his red-bearded face.

Beyond the young soldier, Duke was running straight west through the brush, toward where a stecl dust mustang stood eyeing the man warily. Duke had lost his hat, and his yellow hair swung wildly across his broad, sun-bronzed back.

Fargo jogged around the staked soldier, wincing at the stabbing pain of the arrow in his shoulder, and raised the .36. Aiming quickly as Duke leaped onto the steel dust's back, he squeezed the trigger.

Dust puffed behind the horse's swishing tail.

The horse lunged forward, nearly throwing Duke backward. Clutching the rope reins, Duke glanced at Fargo, then grabbed the steel dust's dancing mane as the horse broke into a ground-eating gallop, heading west.

Fargo drew a bead on the man's bare back, squeezed the trigger, but the hammer pinged on an empty chamber.

Cursing, Fargo wheeled and ran back toward the ravine.

Behind him, the soldier shouted, "Hey, cut me loose, mister!"

"Hold on, soldier!"

The Trailsman pulled the Schuetzen out of the ravine by its barrel, ran back past the writhing, cursing soldier, making sure the muzzle-loader was ready for firing. He dropped to a knee, snugged the Schuetzen's deep-curved, silver-fitted butt-plate to his shoulder, raised the rear leaf site, and sighted down the long, polished barrel.

Duke was a good two hundred yards away and dwindling into the distance, horse and rider bounding up a gradual rise.

Fargo adjusted the sites for the distance, snugged his cheek to the stock. Quivering from the pain in his left shoulder, he lowered the rifle, took a deep breath, fought the pain from his consciousness, and raised the rifle once more.

He had time for only one shot. If he missed, Duke would be out of range by the time Fargo could ram another ball down the rifle's barrel.

The Trailsman lined up the front and rear sights on Duke's back, barely the size of a moth wing from this distance, and dwindling with each passing second. Holding his breath, relaxing against the lightning searing his shoulder, he held the rifle still, and took up the slack in his trigger finger.

Ka-boom!

The Schuetzen's butt-plate slammed against his right shoulder, though he felt it more in the one from which the arrow protruded. He lowered the rifle, blinked against the wafting powder smoke.

One, two, three seconds passed.

Duke continued galloping up the rise. He turned his head slightly as the rifle's blast reached his ears, then threw up his right arm in the Assiniboine victory wave, and turned forward.

Fargo gritted his teeth. "Shit!"

Less than ten feet from the crest of the distant rise, nearly four hundred yards away, Duke's head jerked suddenly forward, both arms flying straight out from his body. The lieutenant sagged down toward the lunging horse's right shoulder, then, as the horse crested the rise, buck-kicking fearfully, rolled off the steel dust's side, hit the ground on his right shoulder, tumbled head over heels, and slammed against a boulder. As the horse crested the rise and disappeared down the other side, Lieutenant Duke fell in a heap at the base of the rock, unmoving.

Hooves thudded to Fargo's right, and he turned to see a brave gallop straight past him toward the rise. "Yem-seen!" the warrior cried, crouched over his bloody midsection, ramming his moccasined heels against the lunging pinto's flanks.

Fargo let the heavy Schuetzen sag to the ground, then fell back on his heels, pain and nausea overwhelming him. He kept his eyes on the wounded brave until, having inspected Duke's body, the brave continued shouting incoherently as he crested the rise and disappeared in the direction of the Indian village.

"You get him?"

Fargo turned. The young bearded soldier regarded him desperately, face etched with pain.

Fargo nodded as he gained his feet, groaning, and plucked a tomahawk from the belt of one of the dead warriors. He'd no sooner chopped the soldier's limbs free of the buried stakes than he turned, cast one more glance in the direction of the dead lieutenant, and passed out.

17

Fargo had no idea how long he was out before he opened his eyes and found himself staring at a woman's deep cleavage—the breasts pushing up from a wine red corset edged with white lace. The deep gap between the pale, lightly freckled breasts rose and fell slowly, moved toward Fargo slightly, and then a woman's voice said, "How do the stitches look, Doctor?"

From Fargo's left a man said, "They seem to be holding fine, and no sign of infection yet."

There was the sound of a cork being popped from a bottle, and then Fargo's left shoulder was set ablaze. He jerked and lifted his head, sucking air through his teeth.

"Skye," Valeria said, gently pushing him back down on the bed. "No sudden movements, or you'll tear the sutures!"

"Do as the young lady says, Mr. Fargo." The doctor whom Fargo had seen earlier—tall, older, with iron gray hair pulled back in a ponytail, pince-nez glasses perched on his broad, pitted nose—rose from a straight-back chair on Fargo's left. He dropped a bottle in a leather grip. "That's a nasty arrow wound, and I had to stitch both sides—a good thirty sutures, all told."

"Ah, shit," Fargo rasped, feeling the deep, burning ache in his upper left chest. He glanced around the long room, both walls of which were lined with a dozen or so beds, most of them filled. Fort Clark's infirmary. "How long before I'm back on my feet?"

"At least a week. The arrow didn't hit anything vital, but it tore you up pretty good. The soldiers got you here about fifteen minutes before you would have bled to death." The doctor snapped the grip closed, donned a ratty beaver hat, nodded at Valeria standing on the right side of Fargo's bed, and began moving down the long alley between the beds, toward the open front door.

Fargo turned to Valeria. Except for a little sunburn and a few small abrasions on her cheeks, she looked as fresh as the day he'd first met her at the steamboat docks in Mandan. "How long I been here?"

"Two days. Don't you remember riding in with the soldiers? The guards said you looked like a dead man riding through those gates. You no sooner told them where they'd find me and Mr. Charley than you passed out." Valeria sat down beside him, smoothed his sweat-damp hair back from his forehead, and gazed softly into his eyes. "Can I get you anything?"

Fargo glanced down at her bosom pushing against his shoulder and, in spite of the fire in his chest, felt the old, stubborn twitch in his loins.

"I mean, within reason!" she scolded, whispering so the men around them couldn't hear.

Fargo felt his mouth corners quirk a grin, and then he glanced around the room once more, where a couple of uniformed men stood or sat beside the white-sheeted lumps of their wounded comrades. "Prairie Dog make it?"

"Of course, I made it, you idiot!"

Fargo turned to see Prairie Dog Charley occupying the bed left of his, lying belly down and looking for all the world like an old, bald, grizzled bear under the white hospital sheets and green wool blankets. Propped on his elbows, he was studying the miniature chess set on the bed before him. "And I wanna know how come you got my dear sweet Brunhilda so damn scratched up! Christ almighty, son, you know how much grease it's gonna take to bring out her shine again?"

Mention of the Schuetzen reminded Fargo of Duke.

"Am I dreaming, or did your dear Brunhilda really blow out the crazy lieutenant's lamp?"

Fingering a pawn and wincing as he adjusted his position in the bed, Prairie Dog nodded. "He's colder'n a grave digger's ass and snugglin' with the snakes right outside these very walls. A patrol hauled him back—or what was left of him after the coyotes had their say."

The old scout chuckled. "And the old major . . . uh, excuse me, Miss . . . *Major Howard* knew what he was talkin' about. Killin' that crazy officer seems to have taken the starch out of the Injuns' shorts. The patrol that came back this mornin' said they saw no Injun sign, and the village beyond Squaw Creek was plum *gone*. Vanished. All that's left are some tracks, ashes, and circles of dead grass where the lodges stood."

"How 'bout the soldiers that helped you spring me and Valeria?"

Prairie Dog cursed and shook his head. "Only two made it—the boy you found staked out by Duke and another holed up in a coulee. Iron Shirt's boys ran the other two down, killed 'em. The boy you found, though, is already back on light wood-cutting duty."

Fargo glanced at Valeria. "Your old man?"

She smiled. "His arrow wound wasn't as bad as yours, and he didn't lose as much blood, so he should be on his feet in a day or two. He's sent couriers out with requests for more men to garrison Fort Clark and to rebuild Fort William."

"Lost nearly a third of our own garrison in that last attack," Prairie Dog growled.

"Figured as much." Fargo groaned as fresh pain stabbed him. "Did the doc leave any whiskey hereabouts? I sure could use a shot."

"He didn't leave any," Prairie Dog said, reaching under his bed. "But I got some."

"With as much blood as you both lost?" Valeria cried, rushing around the bed and plucking the corked brown bottle from the old trapper's hand. "I should say not!"

She shook her head like an admonishing schoolmarm, shifting her gaze between both beds, holding the bottle as though it were an evil talisman. "I'll just hold on to this for six or seven days or when the doctor thinks you're ready for spirituous liquid. Now, you both need to rest. I'll be back in a couple of hours to check on you."

Both Fargo and Prairie Dog watched her bottom sway behind the long, green skirt as she stalked off toward the door, holding the whiskey bottle before her with both hands. Her sunset red hair spilled down her back in swirling curls.

"Ain't right—takin' a man's whiskey," Fargo complained.

"Nope," Prairie Dog said. "But it's hard to argue with a girl that fills out a set o' frillies like that. I wish my memory wasn't as bad as my hearing and my eyesight, and I could remember how she looked without no clothes on!"

"I'd remind you," Fargo said, fatigue washing over him. He lay his head back on the pillow, crossed his hands on his belly, and smiled at the image behind his eyelids. "But I'm afraid you'd have a stroke."

LOOKING FORWARD!
The following is the opening
section of the next novel in the exciting
Trailsman **series from Signet:**

THE TRAILSMAN #317
MOUNTAIN MYSTERY

The Colorado Rockies, 1861—where
a river of death brought men to ruin.

It was not quite noon when Skye Fargo discovered he was being followed. Drawing rein, he shifted in the saddle and scanned his back trail. His lake blue eyes narrowed. A big man, broad of shoulder and narrow of waist, he wore buckskins and a white hat caked with the dust of many miles. A red bandanna added a splash of color. A Colt with well-worn grips was in his holster, a Henry rifle nestled snug in his saddle scabbard.

Fargo did not see anyone but he had learned to trust his instincts. Since daybreak he had been winding along a seldom-used trail that was taking him deep into the heart of the Sawatch Range.

Thick timber hemmed the trail. Ahead rose the towering peaks of the central Rockies, as remote and untamed a region as anywhere on the continent. The haunt of wild beasts and scarcely less wild men, it had yet to be explored. Even the gold seekers, that greedy horde that poured into the Rocky Mountains in 'fifty-eight and 'fifty-nine, had not penetrated this far.

Fargo was in his element. He liked untamed country. He got a thrill out of venturing where few ever set foot. The dangers that gave others pause did not deter him. He considered them an ordinary part of frontier life.

But that did not mean Fargo let himself grow careless. Far from it. His senses were second to none, and his keen ears had detected, faint and far back, the dull thud of a heavy hoof.

Fargo gigged his Ovaro into the spruce and pines, drew rein, and placed his right hand on his Colt.

It could be hostiles. A small tribe known as the Untilla claimed that region as their own, and they resented white intrusion. In the early days a few trappers had gone into their land in search of beaver and were never seen again.

It could be outlaws. The Sawatch Range was a haven for lawbreakers anxious to avoid a noose. They stayed deep in the mountains, coming out from time to time to kill, plunder, and rape.

It could simply be a fellow frontiersman. But another lesson Fargo had learned was to never, ever take anything for granted. A person lived longer that way.

The minutes crawled on a snail's belly. Somewhere a raven cawed. Then a squirrel chattered irately, telling Fargo that whoever was behind him was close. Hunching over the saddle horn, Fargo tensed, his gaze glued to the trail.

Around the last bend came a rider, a greasy beanpole in filthy buckskins and a floppy brown hat. Stubble specked his poor excuse for a chin. He had brown, watery eyes and a wide nose out of all proportion to his scarecrow face. His sorrel was coated with as much dust as Fargo's Ovaro. In the crook of his elbow he cradled a rifle. At his mount's side trotted a large hound with floppy ears.

Fargo was set to jab his spurs against the pinto when another rider appeared.

The second man was stocky and had a thatch of corn-colored hair. He, too, wore buckskins. His, too, were filthy. He wore a blue cap, his sole vanity, and had a bowie in a belt sheath.

Again Fargo went to show himself. A third rider gave him brief pause. Anger gripped him, and he mentally swore.

The third rider was a woman. Curly black hair spilled over her slender shoulders, framing a face that by any standard was uncommonly lovely. Emerald eyes roved over the spectacular scenery with the childlike wonder of someone new to the mountains. Her riding outfit and boots were clean and well kept. She wore a pearl-handled Remington butt-forward on her left hip.

Fargo let them go by. Then he reined the Ovaro onto the trail behind them. "Some folks don't have the brains of a tree stump."

Startled, the woman shifted in her saddle, her hand dropping to her Remington. "Oh, it's you!" she exclaimed.

Her two soiled escorts also whirled and started to level their rifles. The hound uttered a growl and then was silent.

"Fargo!" the beanpole in the lead blurted.

"Cyst," Fargo responded curtly. He focused on the female. "I can't wait to hear your excuse."

Her cheeks flushing, the young woman did not answer right away. When she did, her voice held a note of resentment. "The last I heard, this is a free country."

"We will carve that on your headstone," Fargo said.

"Poppycock!" the woman declared. "You are trying to scare me, just like you did before. But I did not listen then and I will not be intimidated now. I have come too far, invested too much time and money."

Fargo gigged the Ovaro up next to her bay and met her glare with one of his own. "You are too damn contrary for your own good, Mabel Landry."

Her back stiffening, Mabel said heatedly, "I will thank you to use a civil tongue in the presence of a lady. And I will remind you that it is my brother who has gone missing. I am entitled to do as I see fit in my quest to learn his fate."

"If you planned all along to come this far, why did you bother to hire me?" Fargo asked.

"Because everyone says you are the best," Mabel answered frankly. "The best scout, the best tracker, the best at living off the land. If anyone can find Chester, it is you." She paused. "And if you will recall, I asked to come with you but you would not let me. If anyone deserves to be called pigheaded, I suggest that you merit the title more than I."

Fargo sighed. Yes, she had badgered him about coming along, and he had refused, for her own good. That was back in Denver, where she had approached him about searching for her sibling, who went off into the mountains over a year ago and had not been heard from since. "Maybe I should give you back the five hundred dollars and we will go our separate ways with no hard feelings."

Mabel Landry's features softened. "Please. No. That is not necessary. I still wish to retain your services. All I ask is that we hunt for him together."

Frowning, Fargo stared off at the high peaks. Several were mantled with snow even though it was summer. To the northwest reared the highest, Mount Elbert. He had read a newspaper that claimed it was over fourteen thousand feet high. Almost three miles up into the sky.

"Well?" Mabel prompted.

Fargo looked at her. She had come this far, and she would not go back. That she refused to heed his advice rankled, but it was her life to throw away if she wanted. He mentioned as much.

"You are terribly melodramatic, do you know that?" Mabel criticized. "Nothing has happened to me yet, and I suspect nothing will. The tales people spin about the perils to be found out here are greatly exaggerated, in my opinion."

"Your opinion is worthless," Fargo said. "But since you are so determined to get yourself killed, I reckon I might as well do what I can to keep you alive for as long as I can."

"Your compassion overwhelms me," Mabel said sarcastically. But she grinned as she said it.

Fargo nodded at Cyst and Cyst's stocky companion. "What about these two?"

"What about them?" Mabel rejoined. "I hired them to bring me to the settlement you told me about."

"I never said Skagg's Landing was a settlement," Fargo set her straight. There were a few cabins and a trading post; that was it.

"Whatever it is, it is the last place my brother wrote me from, and the logical place to start looking for him in earnest."

"I do not need helpers," Fargo said.

"I paid Mr. Cyst and Mr. Welt in advance to bring me to Skagg's Landing," Mabel said, "so they might as well go with us the rest of the way. Particularly since we are only a day out, or so they have told me."

Fargo frowned.

"What is the matter?" Mabel asked. "You act as if you do not like them. But they have brought me all the way from Denver and been perfect if crude gentlemen." She smirked at him. "You do not have a monopoly on trustworthiness, you know."

"You sure have a way with words," Fargo complimented her.

"Don't avoid the issue. I insist Mr. Cyst and Mr. Welt accompany us as far as the Landing. That is, if they want to."

Cyst was quick to say, "Oh, we want to, ma'am. Turning around and heading back now would be pointless." He grinned, displaying yellow teeth. "Besides, our horses will need a few days to rest up."

"That they will," Welt echoed.

Fargo would as soon shoot them where they sat but he was not a cold-blooded killer. It came from having something Cyst and Welt did not: a conscience. That Mabel had made it this far was no small wonder. "You two ride in front of me at all times."

Welt's jaw muscles twitched. "I take that as an insult, mister."

"Take it any damn way you want," Fargo responded.

Once more Cyst was quick with his tongue. "That's all right, Welt. It is just his style. It does not mean anything."

"The hell it doesn't." Welt would not let it drop. "I know when I am being called no-account and I do not like it." He started to level his rifle.

Just like that, Fargo's Colt cleared leather. The click of the hammer turned Welt to stone. "How dumb are you?"

Mabel Landry made a sniffing sound. "Honestly, now. Was that really called for?"

"I am not fond of being shot," Fargo informed her.

Cyst had also frozen but now he forced a smile, and coughed. "Maybe you are right. Maybe riding together isn't a good idea. How would it be if Welt and I rode on to Skagg's Landing by ourselves? That is, if Miss Landry has no objection."

"I paid you to take me the entire way," Mabel said, "but under the circumstances, yes, perhaps you should ride on."

"I am not giving back any of my share of the money," Welt said sullenly while staring at the muzzle of Fargo's Colt.

"You may keep it," Mabel said.

Cyst beamed. "Fine." He gestured at Fargo. "Until we meet again." To the hound he said, "Heel, Devil!" then flicked his reins.

Fargo let them ride off. Short of shooting them, he had no grounds to stop them. When they were out of sight he twirled the Colt into his holster and clucked to the Ovaro. Within a few yards Mabel Landry was alongside him, and she was not pleased.

"I hope you are happy."

"To be shed of them? Yes."

"You were rude," Mabel criticized. "Those men did nothing to you yet you treated them like they were scum."

"They are," Fargo said.

"Oh really? And what, pray tell, do you know about them that I do not? Or do you base your opinion on nothing but thin air?"

Fargo was tired of her smug attitude. "Cyst has been in these mountains for going on five years now. He drifts where he pleases, and wherever he goes, people have a habit of turning up dead with their pokes missing."

"If that is true," Mabel challenged, "why hasn't he been caught and put on trial?"

"The law can't arrest someone on a hunch," Fargo said. "They need cause, and Cyst always has an alibi."

Mabel was still not satisfied. "If he is as dangerous as all that, why am I still alive? They could have killed me a hundred times over."

"You paid them in advance," Fargo reminded her.

"Implying they already had most of my money," Mabel said. "But I still have a hundred dollars on me, and they are aware of the fact. Why didn't they slit my throat one night while I slept, and help themselves?"

"It is a mystery," Fargo admitted.

"Do you know what I think?" Mabel asked, and then did not wait to hear what he thought. "I think you overreacted. I think you unjustly accuse Mr. Cyst of crimes he did not commit. I think that when you see him again, you owe him an apology."

"And I think that is as likely to happen as it is for gold to grow on trees," Fargo replied.

Mabel snorted. "You might well be the best at what you do but you are awful short on humility. The mature thing to do when you make a mistake is to own up to it."

Fargo was tempted to give her a piece of his mind, and then some. She was a fountain of ignorance, an accident waiting to happen. That she had made it this far was more luck than anything else—luck, and whatever mysterious reason Cyst had for not doing her in. Which reminded him. "How soon after I left Denver did you head out after me?"

"Oh, not more than a couple of hours," Mabel said. "I was furious when you refused to bring me, and I marched down to the stable to hire a horse to come after you. Mr. Cyst and Mr. Welt happened to be there, overheard me talking to the stable owner, and offered to escort me."

"So you did not have it planned in advance?"

"Goodness, no. I had expected to come with you, if you will remember." Mabel ducked under a limb that jutted out over the trail. "Ironic, is it not? Were Mr. Cyst as evil as you claim, and if he had murdered me along the way, my death would be your fault for not letting me ride with you."

"You should have stayed in Denver," Fargo said. "At least there you would be safe."

"Oh, posh. You fret too much over trifles."

"You are as green as grass," Fargo said.

"You can quit trying to scare me," Mabel told him. "I am as safe here as I would be anywhere."

No sooner were the words out of her ruby red mouth than the undergrowth rustled and out ambled a black bear.

No other series packs this much heat!

THE TRAILSMAN

**Available wherever books are sold or at
penguin.com**